MAX MAGIC

MAX MAGIC

STEPHEN MULHERN

with **TOM EASTON** ♠ illustrated by
Begoña Fernández Corbalán

Piccadilly
PRESS

For Philip, who taught me to
keep rowing the boat – T.E.

First published in Great Britain in 2022 by
PICCADILLY PRESS
4th Floor, Victoria House, Bloomsbury Square
London WC1B 4DA
Owned by Bonnier Books
Sveavägen 56, Stockholm, Sweden
www.piccadillypress.co.uk

A CIP catalogue record for this book is available from the British Library.

ISBN: 978-1-80078-379-9
Signed edition ISBN: 978-1-80078-431-4
Also available as an ebook and in audio

1

Interior ⬚ ... ... Begoña ... rnández Corbalán
... ... © Shutterstock
... author photograph © @Oliver_Rosser (... ... Creative
Printed and b... ... ... by ... Grays ... ... cograf S.p.A.

... ... Press is an imprint of ... ... ks UK

Hello to every young person who is about to read my first-ever book – thank you so much.

I also just want to say to you: please never stop believing in yourself and always remember anything is possible.

I have had some of the biggest mountains to climb and a lot of people said things were not possible when I knew they were.

Nobody can ever stop your dreams coming true so don't ever let them try!

Anything Is Possible

Anything Is Possible.

I've always thought that. There are too many people in the world who want to say no. People who want to stop you doing the things you dream about. People who tell you that you can't be successful if you don't talk posh, or that you'll never

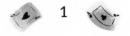 1

get anywhere if you're no good at school. Or that you'll never reach your dreams however hard you try.

I have always believed that anything is possible, no matter how hard things are. I have also always believed in real magic, making the impossible possible! I've seen things and done things that are unbelievable.

In many ways I'm just an ordinary kid, with an ordinary life, in an ordinary world. But there is something special about me too. Something different. Something extraordinary. And if you read on, I'll tell you about it. About how it all started, and how it all ended up.

Let's start at the beginning. I'm Max, Max Mullers. Sometimes people call me Max Magic. One day I hope they'll call me Max the Magnificent, but I'm not quite there yet. I live with my mum, my dad, my brothers Chris and Vinny and my sister Susie in a little terraced house on a busy square in East London. It's crowded and noisy and full of life, and I love it.

The Mullers like to talk. In fact we never shut up. Dad works a toy stall in the market, and he keeps up his patter twenty-four hours a day. He's a proper Cockney geezer. He wears a waistcoat and looks like a cross between Bradley Walsh and Harry Redknapp.

Mum likes a chat too. She works on the phones at the local hospital and knows everyone in the neighbourhood. She's always there with a bit of advice and a word of support.

Vinny loves his football, our family and Major Drumstick's fried chicken. In that order. And he'll talk your ear off about all three if you'll let him. Chris is the mechanic of the family. He's always pulling things apart and putting them back together again and he'll give you a running commentary while he's doing it, even though it's all gobbledegook to the rest of us. As for my sister, well, the only time Susie isn't talking on her phone is when she's asleep. And sometimes she even talks in her sleep. Susie is well into beauty treatments and gives great massages. She works in a salon and keeps up the chatting there 24/7.

Even my dog Lucky likes to get involved in the nattering. He's old and doesn't bark a lot, but he's always yowling and whining and ruffing and grumbling. I often think

he's genuinely trying to talk to me. I'd love to know what he is saying. Probably 'Feed me!'

And me? Well, I'm not too bad at the old rabbiting myself. My teacher used to give me detentions because I was always talking in class, but after a while she gave up and told me it's just background noise to her now. Like traffic, or birds. Well, you've got to be able to talk a bit, don't you? If you're going to be in showbiz?

And I **am** going to be in showbiz. One day, when I'm Max the Magnificent, I'll invent a magic trick so extraordinary that they'll put it in the Museum of Magic in Paris, just next to the enormous statue of me. That's the plan anyway. Dunno what the trick is going to be yet. But it will be **unbelievable!**

The most important thing to know about me is that I have always **loved** magic. It runs in our family – Gran and Grandpa were stage magicians back in the day. I'll tell you more about them later. The point is, Gran taught Dad loads of tricks when he was little. She says he always had a real gift for magic and that he could have been one of the greats. But for some reason he didn't follow in her footsteps. He never went onstage at all – I guess he was more interested in selling stuff. He was still pretty good and he'd always get out his

tricks at parties or Christmas and often used his skills to help him sell toys on the stall. And when I was old enough, Dad started teaching me. The first trick he showed me was how to palm a coin. Now, a magician isn't supposed to reveal the trick behind the magic, but you seem pretty trustworthy, so I'll tell you how to do it, if you promise to keep it to yourself.* It works best with a biggish coin, like a two-pound piece. You press it into the palm of your hand and squeeze your thumb in so the fleshy part of your palm holds the coin in place. You can then turn your hand palm down without the coin dropping out. Next you pretend to throw it into the other hand, quickly closing

* Turn to the back of the book to learn this trick!

it into a fist. The audience is surprised when you open the fist and it's empty. Then you pass the hand with the coin above it and drop the coin, closing it into a fist again. When you reopen your hand, this time the coin is there!

'Show me another trick,' I said, once I thought I had it.

But Dad shook his head. 'Practise that one first,' he said. 'Once you have it perfect, then we'll move on to the next.'

So I did. Every day after school I'd go up to my bedroom in our little terraced house in Coronation Square and I'd practise and practise and practise. It never felt like work. I loved it, especially when

 9

I knew I was getting better.

And then one day, when I was sure I really had it, I showed Dad and I got it just perfect.

He nodded and took out a packet of cards from his inside pocket. 'Let me show you the Floating Card Trick,' he said.

It was then that I decided that one day I was going to be a magician, a real magician, and I was going to perform in front of huge audiences just like Gran and Grandpa had. And my tricks were going to be so good that no one would ever be able to tell how they were done.

Over the next couple of years I learned trick after trick. Some I perfected in a few days; others took me weeks. The Mongolian Rope Trick took me three months! But I kept going. Practise, practise, practise!

Now, every Sunday Gran comes over for dinner, and before pudding I'll show everyone my latest trick. I'll pull a string of colourful napkins from Susie's handbag, I'll whip an egg from behind Chris's ear, I'll read Vinny's mind and tell him what card he was thinking of, I'll pour water from an empty jug (and sometimes this trick will even work and I **won't** soak Mum's new trousers). I love the look of astonishment on people's faces when the trick goes well, and I've learned how to make a joke out of it when it goes wrong.

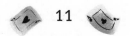

Gran says I'm a born performer. Dad says I'm a born clown. But a good magician needs to be a little bit of both.

Last Sunday was a particularly memorable one. After we'd finished eating I got everyone to push their chairs back a bit from the table.

'I have a new magic trick!' I announced.

'Very nice, dear,' Gran said, beaming at me.

Some of the other members of the family were a little less enthusiastic. Dad peered at me suspiciously over his glasses. He always dresses properly for dinner, in his Sunday suit.

'Don't make a mess, will you?' Mum

called. She was fussing about with the dessert spoons next door in the little kitchen.

'Do you want to see the trick or not?' I asked her. 'Cos you're going to need to come in here.'

'Will I end up with wet legs?' she asked as she came into the dining room a bit reluctantly. 'These are new trousers.'

'That only happened once,' I said, arranging dessert bowls around the table. 'The jug slipped.'

'Will you break a window?' Vinny asked without looking up. He was reading a football magazine, which he technically wasn't allowed to do during Sunday lunch.

'That wasn't my fault,' I pointed out, glancing at the cracked pane in the sitting-room window.

'You're not going to knock the clock off the wall again, are you?' Chris asked. 'It took me an hour to fix it last time. At least I think it was an hour. Hard to tell when the clock's broken.'

'I'm not going anywhere near the clock,' I said impatiently. 'The dresser fell over.' It was a painful memory. I had to go to A & E cos I got bashed on the bonce when I tried to stop it.

I set out fresh glasses for me, Mum, Dad, Gran, Chris, Vinny and Susie, who was chatting to someone on her phone, which she technically wasn't allowed to do during Sunday lunch.

'Will you break my watch again?' Dad asked with a pained frown. Sometimes I wonder if he regrets starting me off on magic in the first place.

'No, no hammers involved in this trick,' I said, filling the glasses with water. 'And that watch was slow anyway. I was doing you a favour.' I put the jug right in the middle of the table, then added a vase of flowers from the windowsill as an afterthought.

'Look, stop talking, everyone,' I said. 'Susie, stop chatting for two secs. Chris, pay attention for two secs. Vinny, stop

reading for two secs. Mum, sit down for two secs. Dad, stop frowning. Honestly, this trick will definitely work and nothing will get smashed. You lot are unbelievable!'

Finally everyone settled down, stopped what they were doing and watched me.

'Right,' I said. I grinned and seized two corners of the tablecloth. 'It's all in the wrist,' I explained with a wink. *'DOOSH!'*

I whipped the cloth away in a blur, leaving everything still standing neatly on the table.

Or at least . . . that was what was supposed to happen. Instead, the cutlery flew off in all directions, sending Chris and Vinny ducking for cover. Lucky yelped and shot out the door in a mad panic, Susie squealed as the dessert bowls shot across the room, smashing into the dresser and knocking the clock off the wall. And seven glasses of water spun towards Mum, drenching her from head to toe.

There was silence as everyone glared at me. Everyone except Gran, who was cackling away in delight.

'I think I know what went wrong,' I said, after a moment. 'Let me try that again. It's all in the **other** wrist.'

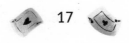 17

I like to show off my magic tricks at
school too. I just love it when a crowd of
pupils gathers round, watching me make
coins disappear or read people's minds.
Sometimes I wish I could really read
people's minds. Because then I could read
my friend Sophie's mind during maths
tests. Sophie's really smart.

Me? Maybe not so much.

Most things in my life are great,
fantastic, fabulous. MAGIC!

But some things aren't quite so good.
Like school, and schoolwork, schoolteachers
and school bullies. Yeah, it's mostly school-
related things I'm not too keen on. I'm
not sure I'll ever actually learn anything

 19

at school – I'm too busy chatting. But you never know. Anything is possible!

Even school has its good points. That's where I met my best friends, like Sophie and Stretch and Daisy. And school is where I like to test out my magic tricks on unsuspecting fellow pupils.

Being able to do magic is useful, as well as fun. Magic can get you out of a sticky spot.

The thing is, my school is a little bit . . . well, rough. There are fights in the playground most days, and that's just the teachers. I've got some great friends there, but my school has more than its fair share of bullies too. Sometimes at school it seems as though the bullies outnumber the nice kids and might run out of people to bully and have to bully each other. That's not a bad idea actually. Can we just get the bullies to bully each other and leave the rest of us alone? Something to think about.

Anyway, most people have their own way of dealing with bullies. Some hide away in the library, some fight back, some people join the bullies and do a bit of bullying themselves, some people hand over their lunch money and shrug.

Me? I use magic.

Before school, at break time, at lunchtime and after school, I'm somewhere

 21

in the playground doing tricks, finding
eggs behind people's ears, palming coins,
flipping cards, practising my patter. Even
the bullies stop bullying for a while and
watch me.

At least most of them do.

All except one.

George Bottley.

The worst bully of them all. Some
bullies are clever and sly. Some bullies are
angry and stupid. Bottley is just mean.
Big and mean. Not particularly stupid, not
particularly sly. Just mean.

The other day he picked me up off the
ground with one hand. My little legs were
kicking away at thin air.

'Why are you always picking on me?' I managed to squeak.

'You wanna know why I give you a hard time, Mullers?'

I nodded.

Maybe he was having trouble at home, I thought. Or he was being bullied by someone even bigger. The Hulk, maybe?

 23

Perhaps if we could just talk about his problem, we could break the cycle of anger.

He leaned in close and grinned. 'It's because I like it!'

So much for breaking the cycle of anger. The only things likely to get broken were my legs.

Bottley is built like a big ape. A gorilla, or a baboon, or one of those ones with the red face and the blue bum. Or is it the other way around? Anyway, he has long arms and huge hairy hands. He has hair growing out of his nose, hair growing out of his ears, hair growing out of his neck. He probably has hair growing on his big blue bum too, but I don't want to find out.

Do you want to know what Bottley's special bullying tactic is?

Worms.

He is **obsessed** with worms. His dad is a keen fisherman and gets George to help him dig up worms to use as bait. George likes to take some of these worms and put them in the pockets of this big old yellow coat he always wears. And if you're unlucky enough to be caught by George Bottley, then he'll hold you down, and he won't let you up until you close your eyes, open your mouth . . .

And then he'll drop a worm right in. I told you he was horrible, didn't I? Bottley is immune to magic. He just

doesn't care. Imagine being the sort of person who has no curiosity, no wonder, no need to find out how that trick was done. Or to ask where did that card go? Or can I have my coin back? Or why did you pour water on my trousers?

A person like that has no soul. Nothing inside but emptiness.

It's not as if I haven't tried. After weeks of Bottley shoving my head down the toilet, and chewing on worms (and me a fussy eater!), or being on the receiving end of a double-atomic wedgie in front of my friends, I had turned, in desperation, to magic.

Remember that the first trick Dad ever

taught me was palming a coin? When Bottley
cornered me behind the bike racks one time,
out of sight of the teachers, I thrust my
hands into my pockets and found a pound. I
palmed it and pulled my hands out.

'Wait, wait,' I said as Bottley advanced,
lifting his hairy knuckles off the ground just
long enough to crack them. 'Let me show
you something.'

Bottley stopped and eyed me
suspiciously. I reached behind his filthy
ear and pulled out a shiny pound coin. The
bully's eyes widened.

'Thanks,' he grunted, and snatched the
coin out of my fingers. 'You can do that
again tomorrow.'

 27

Bottley, of course, wasn't interested in the magic. He just wanted the coin, and I couldn't afford to buy my freedom with a pound coin every day. So I tried to avoid him as much as I could. Every day was like filming one of those nature documentaries where they're trying to track down some big gorilla in the rainforest. I had to learn about the gorilla's routine, his patterns of behaviour, what time he ate and what time he went to the loo. Lots of details I didn't really want to know, if I'm honest. But unlike in a nature documentary, I was trying to **avoid** the gorilla.

Yeah, Bottley was a problem.

But when I think back to when this all

started, and to the day my life changed forever, I can see, in a funny way, that it was Bottley who set everything off. Bottley who started the trouble. And Bottley who helped me find the solution. The magic. You'd never think of Bottley as someone who could make something good happen. Someone who could make magic happen.

But hey, anything is possible, right?

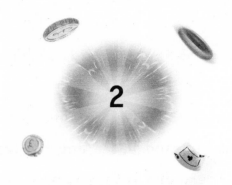

2

The Day of Destiny

That day, the day it all began, started
just like any other day. I woke to the
thrilling sound of thunder and rushed
to my window, overlooking Coronation
Square, only to find that the rumbling
noise was Mrs Singh next door taking out
the bins. There was no rain. In fact, it

was looking like it was going to be a lovely day.

Coronation Square is a noisy place. There are cars and buses and bin lorries outside. There are always people shouting and talking and playing music in the square itself. There are the Singhs next door to the right and the Kellys next door to the left. Both families are big and noisy.

But most of the noise comes from inside our house, to be honest.

As I came downstairs I was hit by a wall of sound. Dad was looking through the post and complaining about the size of the electricity bill. 'How are you all using

31

so much electricity?' he asked. 'Are you eating it?'

But no one was listening to him. Dad was always moaning about money.

Chris was reading out an interesting article he'd seen in 'Popular Mechanics' magazine. But no one was listening to him either. Mechanics wasn't as popular with us as it was with him.

No one was even pretending to listen to Vinny as he discussed the team line-up for West Ham on the weekend. Susie was on the phone talking to one of her friends about another of her friends who'd just had a break-up with yet another one of her friends. Maybe Susie and her friend were listening to each other but I wouldn't have bet on it.

Lucky was doing his half-bark, growling-whining noise thing, which I guess was him explaining to everyone that breakfast was the most important meal of the day and so could he have more of it, please? No one was listening to him either.

Mum was leaning on the kitchen counter, reading out everyone's horoscopes. The horoscopes was the only bit of the paper she was interested in. Mum loves horoscopes and astrology and that sort of thing. She reads a magazine called 'Astral Plane'. Dad says it's all

 33

claptrap and has no scientific basis. She replies that that's just what a Leo would say.

'It says today is going to be a day of destiny for you, Max,' Mum said, peering at her paper. 'A day that will change your life!'

'Just me, or all Aries?' I asked.

'They don't name you. So must be all Aries, I suppose,' Mum said.

'Big day for Aries,' I said. I had a piece of toast and a cup of tea. Then I said goodbye to Lucky and grabbed my school bag. Mum always drops Lucky around at Gran's shop on her way to work, and I pick him up on my way home. It's like he has a job that he has to go to every day, except the job is basically just him sleeping on an old armchair in Gran's back room.

I reckon there are worse jobs.

As I walked out the door, Mum handed me a chocolate bar for my snack and said, 'Have a magical day, Max.'

'I'll do my best!' I replied with a grin.

I don't remember much about what happened at school that day. Except for in history when Mr Fisher asked me where they signed the Magna Carta.

'At the bottom?' I suggested.

Apparently that wasn't the right answer. Got a laugh though! They should give you extra marks for laughs.

 35

I suppose I must have learned something. Maybe in maths? English? Hopefully whatever it was I'd learned would pop back into my head when I needed it, but for now it was all a bit of a blur.

No, the important bit came after school. We were in the playground. I was showing Daisy, Sophie and Stretch a trick. Just a little misdirection with a pack of cards, nothing special.

'Wait, do that again,' Daring Daisy said, frowning.

I winked at her and shuffled the deck, springing the cards from one hand to another with a flutter.

'Again?' I asked with a grin.

'Again!' Daisy repeated determinedly.

'You won't see the trick,' Sophie told
her. 'You never do.'

Stretch grinned. He liked watching me
do tricks and never tried to figure them
out. He's a simple soul, Stretch, and he
doesn't need a lot to be happy. Just a
lovely hot cup of tea. And gymnastics.

He's amazing at gymnastics. He can do back flips, front flips and sideways flips. He can walk on his hands, juggle with anything and climb up walls in a flash. That's how he got his nickname: Seb 'Stretchy' Cross, Gymnastics Boss.

We were sitting on the low wall separating the football pitch from the playground. A couple of kids on their way home stopped to watch as I cut the pack and flipped the top card up to show it. The Queen of Hearts.

'Was this your card?' I asked.

Daisy's mouth dropped open. 'Yes!' she replied, astonished.

Sophie laughed. Sophie is the clever

one out of our gang and she always thinks
she knows how my tricks work, but I don't
think she does.

Stretch murmured in appreciation,
as did the kids who'd stopped to watch.
Everyone knows Max Magic. My reputation
is like my nose. It precedes me.

'But how?' Daisy said. 'Who . . . ?
When . . . ? Wait, do it again.'

Daisy was staring at the cards in my
hands, the same way Lucky might stare at
a piece of sausage.

'Misdirection is the key,' Sophie said
breezily. 'If you look hard enough, you'll
see the trick. So Max will distract you at
the critical moment. He'll make you look

 39

somewhere else while he slips the card he wants out of his sleeve.'

'It works the same way with Lucky,' I said. 'Pretend to throw a sausage and he'll go scampering across the room to look for it while I pop it in my mouth.'

'Exactly,' Sophie said. 'Misdirection.'

'Are you saying I'm as dumb as a dog?' Daisy asked.

'Lucky is a very intelligent dog,' Stretch pointed out.

Daisy gave him a look.

I grinned and did the trick again. This time Daisy picked the Seven of Clubs. I slid it back into the pack. Shuffle, cut, flip. Just at the right moment, I waved one hand in the air and said, **'Doosh!'**

Doosh? Oh, 'doosh' doesn't actually mean anything. It's just something I say. My catchphrase, if you like. Along with **unbelievable!**

Daisy's eyes followed my hand and that's when I switched the card, with my other hand. I held it out. The Seven of Clubs. Another murmur from the people watching. There were more and more of them now, gathering around in a big circle.

'See!' Sophie said, as though she'd seen me switch the card, though I knew she hadn't because she'd also been looking at my waving hand. Everyone had.

 41

'Wait. Do it again,' Daisy said . . . again. She had a look of fierce concentration on her face. There's a reason why Daisy's nickname is Daring, and you do have to be on your guard around her. Daisy loves a prank. If you're not careful, you'll find salt in your sugar bowl, clingfilm on your toilet seat or a frog in your pencil case. Her greatest achievement ever was when she put up signs in the loos at school announcing that the paper-towel dispensers were now voice-activated. All day, out in the corridors, you could hear kids screaming, 'PAPER TOWEL, PLEASE!' at the tops of their voices.

I sighed. 'This is the eighteenth time

I've shown you, Daisy,' I said. 'If you haven't spotted how it's done by now, you never will.'

'Then tell me,' Daisy begged. 'Tell me how you do the trick.'

I shook my head and waggled a single eyebrow. Which was something else I'd been practising recently. 'It's not a trick,' I said. 'It's magic.'

'Yep,' Stretch said, shrugging. 'It's magic and that's that.'

Sophie sighed and rolled her eyes. She was about to say something else as I shuffled the cards again. But then I heard the sound of the Great Bells ringing in the Bow Church. It was 5 o'clock.

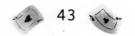 43

'Unbelievable!' I said in alarm. 'I've got to go.'

'There's no such thing as magic,' Sophie was saying as I shoved the cards into one of my pockets. 'Not REAL magic.'

But Max Magic was on the move!

'See you tomorrow,' I cried as I raced off through the crowd.

'Show us another one!' Jamie Thomson shouted.

'Do the coin trick!' Akilah Youssef called.

'No time,' I replied. 'Maybe tomorrow.' I grinned. Always leave 'em wanting more, I thought.

Unfortunately I was about to discover that drawing attention to yourself could sometimes be more trouble than it was worth. As I rounded the corner of the science building, I saw something that made me skid to a stop. I stopped too quickly, in fact, and fell backwards onto my bottom.

From my position there on the cold pavement, I looked up at the thing that had made me stop. The thing was a person. A big, hairy ape-like person. A mean person. A person with muddy, wriggly, wormy pockets in his yellow coat.

Today, it turned out, was not going to be an avoiding day. Bottley laughed and stepped forward menacingly. I was

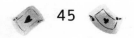

surprised to see him, to be honest, as I'd
never seen Bottley in the playground after
school before. I assumed he went back to
the gorilla enclosure at the zoo to comb
his knuckles. Or the riverbank to look for
worms. But no, here he was.

'You didn't invite me to your little
magic show, Mullers,' he growled. 'I'm very
upset.'

'It wasn't a magic show,' I said. 'Just a
couple of tricks, that's all.'

'I like tricks,' he said, with a twisted
grin. 'In fact, why don't you show me that
trick again? The one where you pull money
out from behind my ear.'

'I don't have any money,' I lied as I got

to my feet. My bottom was a little sore.
I did have a few pound coins tucked away
in my pockets, but I didn't want Bottley to
know that.

'Jump up and down,' he said, leaning his
big, hard head forward.

'What?' I replied, confused.

'Jump up and down,' Bottley repeated.
'Like a little jumpin' bean.'

I shrugged and jumped up and down.

CLINK went the coins.

'Unbelievable,' I muttered, rolling my
eyes.

Bottley grinned.

Could I make a run for it? No. One of
those big, long gorilla arms would probably

stretch out down the street and grab me. And even if I did get away, Bottley would only find me again at school tomorrow. Paying to be left alone wasn't fair, and it wasn't cheap, but it was better than having your head shoved down a toilet, and I didn't fancy eating worms today. I was on a strict no-worm diet.

So I palmed a coin and reached out my hands, waggling them mysteriously.

'Alakazam, alakabash!' I said, rolling my eyes back in my head like I'd seen a sorcerer do on a TV show. Then I reached behind the grinning Bottley's ear and pulled out a coin.

Bottley snatched it.

'Pleasure as always,' I said as I moved to walk away, but Bottley grabbed my wrist and yanked me back.

'And the rest,' Bottley said. 'One coin by itself doesn't clink.'

I looked at the bigger boy and my heart sank. I'd worked hard for this money, helping Dad out on the market stall. I'd been saving up to buy a cloak for my stage act. Maybe it was time to stand up to Bottley.

'No,' I said. 'You've got your pound. And that's all you're going to get.'

As soon as the words came out of my mouth I regretted them.

Bottley's face grew dark, and he yanked

 49

me forward. 'We'll see about that, Mr Magic,' he growled.

Now, I have deep pockets, with lots of things in them. I also have extra pockets. A magician can never have too many places to hide things.

Bottley jammed his hand into one of those deep pockets.

The wrong pocket.

His fingers found something. He pulled it out and looked at what he'd grabbed.

'An egg?' he said, confused. 'I don't want an–'

I don't know what made me do it. There was something in his stupid mean face that spurred me to act. Before he could finish his sentence, I shoved his hand up, crushing the egg against his big, hard forehead. Yolk and egg white splattered everywhere. He lurched back, roaring and wiping the goo and bits of shell out of his eyes.

There was a moment's pause as we both tried to process what had just happened. My mind flashed back to Mum telling me that this was going to be a day of destiny for me. Was my destiny to have my head pulled off by a hairy ape with worms in his pockets?

And then . . .

'I'M GOING TO STOMP YOU FOR THAT, MULLERS!' he roared, and lumbered forward.

There was nothing for it but to RUN.

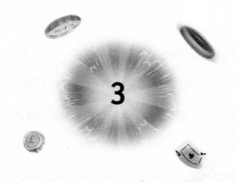

Boomerang Blast!

I raced towards the market. I'm a lot faster than Bottley the Baboon and, just to make sure, I doubled back through the narrow, winding streets of the City until I'd made sure my pursuer was well and truly lost.

I was pretty sure Bottley didn't know I

worked at the market. I'd never seen him around there and Bottley isn't the sort to ask polite questions about your family. And even if he did, you can't answer with worms in your mouth. I ran faster. The bells had stopped ringing a while ago and I knew I was late. I also knew Bottley would come looking for me at school next day to talk about eggs. And worms.

But that was a problem for tomorrow.

Even with all my worries, I felt my mood lift as I dashed between the shoppers wandering the crowded streets. They were looking for a bargain among the brightly coloured market stalls selling everything from genuine leather handbags to genuine fake branded wristwatches. There were hats and crystals, belts and dreamcatchers, shoes and tea sets.

'It's all going cheap today!' I heard a seller crying out. 'None of it's nicked, it's just not paid for!'

'Pound a punnet, pound a punnet!' yelled Mr Fowler from his fruit-and-veg stall as I raced past. 'Mind how you go, Max Magic!'

I waved but didn't stop. I had no time for shopping. I was late!

Mr Grace saw me from behind his fresh fish stall. 'Oi, Max Magic,' he yelled after me, 'pick a cod, any cod!' He roared with laughter and I grinned. Same joke every day.

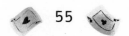

My stomach growled as I breathed in the delicious aromas of Mrs Robinson's vegan pies and the Kowalski family's bakery. There were lots of other things to eat in the market too: whelks and eels, pizza and cheese, sausage and chips.

I passed the Kumars' curry stall. Mrs Kumar frisbeed a poppadom to me as I ran and I snatched it out of mid-air, to the delight of the hungry shoppers in the queue.

'Next time try a samosa!' Mrs Kumar shouted after me.

'I'll think about it!' I called back.

The Kumars are always trying to get me to try something a bit hotter than a poppadom, but the truth is I'm a fussy eater,

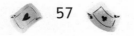

and not just when it comes to worms. Spicy food doesn't sit well with me. Mum tells me to be polite and never say I hate a particular food. Instead I have to say that it's 'not my favourite'. Well, spicy food is definitely not my favourite. But that's the market for you. There's something here for everyone. Everyone's different and not everyone has to like the same thing.

I loved the market. I felt at home here, and safe.

My dad's stall was in the heart of the market, halfway down Petticoat Lane itself. Stallholders came and went; some appeared for just a few days then left again, others were occasional visitors, but Mullers' toy stall had been there in the middle of the market for over thirty years, every day, rain or shine.

I worked the stall on Sunday mornings and every weekday from five to six, while Dad went off for his tea. Dad is usually cheerful and friendly, always first with a kind word and happy to slip a couple of shiny pound coins into your hand. But he is also a man who enjoys his food and if I kept him waiting for his chops and two veg, his good humour could be tested.

I skidded to a stop, panting, in front of the stall at exactly 5.11 p.m. Dad was serving a customer but glanced over and gave me a look.

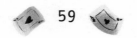 59

I knew that look. Dad's looks could say a lot. Sometimes they were good, sometimes they were fun, and sometimes they were not fun at all. And this one said I was late, and he was hungry.

As I shuffled closer, a weight in my tummy and a guilty look on my face, Dad held out a stack of the latest toys we were selling on the stall: small plastic red, white and blue boomerangs with flashing lights. I loved them – they were fun to throw and easy to sell.

'No need for me to guess where you've been,' Dad said. 'Practising your magic again, lost track of time. Am I right?'

Not wanting to worry him about Bottley, I just nodded and took the stack of boomerangs.

Here's a thing. Dad was the one who first taught me magic. And he loves magic. He always smiles and claps his hands at the shows I put on at Sunday dinner. But I sometimes see him watching

 61

me when I'm practising and I see him put on one of his looks. Like he's frowning a little, and not just when I've broken a vase or set fire to a tea towel. As much as Dad loves magic, he doesn't think it can be a career. He doesn't think it can be your whole life.

'You need to concentrate on selling,' he would say. 'Or studying. I used to think I could be a magician. But at the end of the day, Max, it's all just tricks. Magic isn't real, Max. Concentrate on what's real. What you can hold in your hand.'

I thought he was going to tell me that again today. But he just sighed. Then he ruffled my hair and gave me a wink. 'See you later, Magic Boy. I'll be back to close up at six.'

I nodded and grinned, relieved that Dad wasn't too angry. This was one of my favourite times of the day. It felt great to be given the responsibility to look after the stall and it gave me the chance to show off a bit, which, as you might have realised by now, was one of my favourite things to do! And then, once Dad came back at six, I'd head off to Gran's to pick up Lucky before going home. Gran always had a warm stack of biscuits waiting for me and Lucky to share. My tummy growled again as I thought about them.

But for now, I had a job to do. I felt

the familiar thrill of excitement and nerves as I stepped out in front of the stall. I looked around and spotted my first mark. A young mum with her hair in a ponytail and two neat-looking boys by her side, both in school uniform. With a flick of my wrist I sent a flashing boomerang towards them. It hummed as it went. It shot past the astonished faces of the uniformed boys, swung around and headed back to land safely in my hand.

'Red, white and blue,' I sang. 'They come back to you.'

The boys looked at me, then laughed and dragged their mum over.

'What do you call a boomerang that

won't come back?' I asked them with a
wink. 'A stick!' I whizzed another one
out, this time an inch past the large nose
of a businessman who was inspecting
leather wallets at the stall across the
way.

A small crowd of people had stopped
to watch, smiling. Enjoying the show.
Businesspeople, grans and grandpas,
mums and dads and kids. I spotted a
group of tourists speaking Spanish and
taking photos of me. And I just loved the
attention.

'Hola!' I yelled. That was the only
Spanish I knew, but they looked delighted.
I whizzed out a few more boomerangs.

'Took me ages to figure out how to make one of these come back!' I cried. 'Then it hit me.'

I knew that as soon as a few people stopped to watch then more would come. No one wants to miss out on a free show; everyone wants to know what everyone else is looking at.

'Three in a pack,' I said. 'They all fly back.'

One of the boys in uniform reached out a hand for a boomerang.

'Sorry,' I said, shaking my head. 'I can't give you one just now. They take a bit of practice, you see. Not a lot, but getting the flick of the wrist just right takes a

while. If I give you
one of these and
you throw it without
practising first, you
might hit someone
in the eye and then
the council will come and shut us down.'

The boy looked disappointed. I went
down on my knees to meet him at eye level.

'It's not hard though. If your mum were
to buy a couple of packs, you can take 'em
home, go out in the garden and follow
the instructions. You do that, and . . .
Doosh! I guarantee you'll be bringing
boomerangs back within half an hour. A bit
of practice, you see. A bit of practice and

not giving up. Oh, and a bit of magic. If it don't work, I'll give you your money back, and that's a Max Magic guarantee.'

I winked and offered a fist and the boy bumped it with a grin.

The mum rolled her eyes but smiled and reached for her purse. In seconds I was back up on the trestle table, juggling with three of the boomerangs to the delight of the crowd.

'For a while I forgot how to throw a boomerang,' I said. 'But then it came back to me.'

Mums are the best customers when you work a toy stall. And grans.

I saw an elderly lady standing at the

front, watching me flick out boomerang after boomerang. I hopped down and held one up, then I closed my fingers around it and held out my fist. The lady looked puzzled, then I turned my fist over and opened it to reveal . . . nothing! She blinked in surprise and there was a smattering of applause from the crowd. But I wasn't finished. I reached forward and plucked something from the pocket of her coat. I handed it to her – it was a little flower.

The lady laughed and took out her purse. 'Go on then. I'll have three, please,' she said. 'One for each of my grandchildren.'

Things were going brilliantly! The boomerangs were a smash! Dad would be so pleased with me when I got back. Sometimes a little bit of magic is all you need. The crowd was building now, filling the lane, squashing together like sardines. I hopped back up onto the trestle table to give myself more room and did a little tap dance, which raised a big laugh.

But just then I spotted something unwelcome burst through the crowd.

The unwelcome thing was wearing a yellow coat.

George Bottley smirked at me and, before I could move a muscle, he snatched the stack of boomerangs off the table!

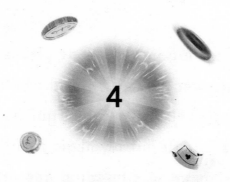

4

Market Mayhem

Zip, twang, bang!

I watched in horror as
Bottley hurled the boomerangs
around the market, sending
punters ducking. One bounced off
Mr Ponsonby the vicar's nose. Another
pinged off a businessman's briefcase.

Bottley was chucking them, not flicking. No finesse, no panache, no style!

'BLUE, WHITE AND RED, THEY'LL HIT YOU IN THE HEAD!' he yelled, hurling half a dozen in quick succession at the group of Spanish tourists, sending them ducking for cover.

At one point he threw three at once. One stuck, quivering, in a watermelon on Mr Fowler's stall, the second smashed a plate on the crockery stand opposite, and the third lodged itself into one of Mrs Robinson's lentil pies, which sort of exploded, sending the filling all over her clean apron. Shrieks and squeals peppered the marketplace.

'QUE PASA?' one of the Spanish tourists wailed.

And then I saw something that made my heart sink quicker than a cardboard submarine.

Strolling through the market like they owned the place (which they sort of did) came the Crayfish Twins. Dad had told me a thousand times to keep clear of the Crayfish Twins. They were proper old-school East End gangster types, he'd said. Don't mess with them, don't argue with them and don't hit them with boomerangs.

He might not have actually said that last one, but it was implied.

The Crayfish Twins didn't look like

twins. One of them was short and stocky,
the other was tall and thin. One was bald,
the other was dark haired. One had an
earring, the other had a nose
ring. The only thing they
had in common was their
dark well-fitting suits. I had
to admit, those boys looked
sharp!

As soon as I saw them, I knew this was going to end badly, but I tried to stop it anyway. Having got to my feet, I lunged towards Bottley as he carried on flinging boomerangs into the crowd, laughing wildly.

'PEW, PEW, PEW!' he shouted.

What an idiot!

I grabbed his arm, he flung one last boomerang and I turned to watch it go.

Time slowed to a crawl.

'Noooooooooo!' I cried as I saw the little flashing object hurtle across the marketplace and hit the taller Crayfish twin, Gary, right in the centre of his forehead.

He fell back, surprised, and crashed into the Kumars' curry stall. Their trestle table's

75

legs collapsed under his weight and he went
down in a cloud of colourful sweet-smelling
spices.

'Ha ha!' Bottley crowed, delighted at
the carnage he'd created. 'I'm outta here.
See you tomorrow, Mullers!' He shoved the
remaining boomerangs back in my hand,

leered at me with a threatening gleam in his eye, then he was gone.

I rushed over to see if I could do anything to help, but Gary Crayfish was already on his feet. He no longer looked like a gangster in a navy suit. He looked like a clown. He had patches of yellow saffron, red paprika and black mustard seed all over him. His head was covered in a brown powder I didn't recognise until he sneezed violently, exploding in a puff of spicy-smelling . . .

'Cumin!' he coughed. 'I'm allergic to cumin!'

Barry plucked something from Gary's chest. A little boomerang, red, white and

 77

blue. Then he turned and saw me standing a few feet away, watching in horror. He looked down at the stack of boomerangs in my hand and compared it to the one he held.

'YOU!' he cried. 'You're the Mullers kid.'

'It wasn't me,' I said, knowing it sounded pathetic.

He stalked over to me. 'Look at my brother's suit,' he snapped. 'That cost £200. You got £200 for a new suit for my brother?'

I shook my head. My heart was pounding. A crowd had gathered to watch. This wasn't the sort of show I'd wanted to be in.

'Well, you'd better find it then, hadn't you?' the man asked softly. Dangerously.

'Y–you could clean it?' I suggested, tentatively.

Barry narrowed his eyes and pointed to the yellow patch on Gary's lapel. 'That's saffron,' he growled. 'You can't get saffron out.'

'Don't talk to him,' a voice said. 'Talk to me.'

'Dad!' I said.

'Mr Mullers,' Gary Crayfish said. 'Your boy here has some explaining to do.'

'It wasn't his fault,' Dad said. 'Mr Kumar called me and explained that some lad in a yellow coat was causing trouble. I came to sort it out.' Dad looked at me and gave me a reassuring smile. Then he turned

79

back to Barry Crayfish and glared. Dad
hated the Crayfish Twins.

'Well, you were too late, Mr Mullers,'
Barry said. 'And now my brother needs a
new suit.'

'I'll take care of that,' Dad said.

'Dad!' I cried. £200 was a lot of
money for us. That stack of bills on the
kitchen dresser wasn't going to take care
of itself.

'And I think he might need a bit of
compensation on top,' Barry said. 'For the
trauma.'

'I need counselling,' Gary agreed. He
sneezed again.

'So shall we say £250?' Barry said.

'£250?!' Dad said.

'No way!' I cried. It wasn't fair. It had been Bottley's fault. Or mine. Now Dad was going to get stung.

Barry looked over at our toy stall. 'Nice stall,' he said, dangerously. 'It would be a shame if something happened to it . . .' He let the threat hang in the air.

Dad breathed in deeply, then he nodded.

Gary sneezed again. 'I feel like I'm in a marinade,' he said.

'You've got three days, Mr Mullers,' Barry said as he led his brother away.

 81

'You don't want to make an enemy of the Crayfish Twins, let me assure you.'

'Dad,' I said, once they'd gone, 'you can't just give him that much money.'

'It's fine, Max,' he said. He ruffled my hair and gave me a cheery grin. But I could see in his eyes that deep down he was worried.

'How can they do this?' I asked, furious at the injustice. 'Who even are the Crayfish Twins?'

'Well, they go round the market taking money from people,' Dad said. 'That's their business.'

'What do they give in return?' I asked.

'They leave you alone,' Dad said. 'If you don't pay up, then stuff happens.'

'What sort of stuff?'

'Things get broken,' Dad said. 'First an awning, then a wheel, then your stock. And finally, they break your arms.'

'Why don't the police do anything?' I asked, astonished.

'They're too clever to do anything in front of the police,' Dad explained. 'Everyone's too scared to say anything. People just pay up because it's easier.'

'It's like Bottley,' I muttered.

'What's that?' Dad asked.

'They're just bullies,' I said. 'The Crayfish Twins are bullies.'

 83

'They are,' Dad said. 'That's exactly what they are.'

Dad and I helped the Kumars clear up the mess. They'd seen the whole thing, so at least they didn't blame me. But there was a lot of clearing up to do. The spices made my eyes water and I felt a choking cough at the back of my throat from the chilli powder hanging in the air. Why did it have to be spices?

What a disaster.

'Sorry, Dad,' I said once we were done.

I'd disappointed him three times today, and that felt worse than anything.

'It wasn't your fault, son,' Dad said.
'Like you said, the Crayfish Twins are
bullies.'

'If only there was something we could
do about them,' I said.

I didn't just mean the twins. I meant
all bullies. All people who steal from you,
just as a price for not hurting you, and
make you feel bad for simply existing.

'Some things you just can't fix.' Dad
sighed. 'And sometimes life isn't fair.'

I knew exactly how Dad felt. Between
us, we now had Bottley and the Crayfish
Twins on our backs.

Who was next? Jack the Ripper?

But I wasn't sure Dad was right when

he said that some things can't be fixed.

I wasn't ready to give up.

Deep in thought and deeply unsettled, I made my way to Gran's shop. As soon as I went in, I felt better.

Gran's shop is my absolute favourite place in the world to be, and not just because Gran lives there. She is small and wrinkled like a walnut, but you shouldn't underestimate her. She's tougher than that walnut and a lot harder to crack. She's also funny, and though she sometimes has a sharp tongue, she's the most loving person. She's always got a tray of biscuits baking away in her tiny kitchen behind the shop, and she's never too busy to listen to your problems and give you advice.

Gran is a proper old East Ender. She talks in rhyming slang and drinks stout and has even been known to eat eels, which are definitely very **not my favourite**. Eels are basically just big river worms and I really hope Bottley never finds out about them.

And Gran was a real live stage magician, long ago. She grew up when half of the East End was still bombed-out buildings after the war. That's when she met my grandad – he was a magician too. They teamed up and became a magical double act! Gran was always ahead of her time.

 87

A real feminist. Come to think of it, Grandad was a feminist too. The two of them were equals in everything. They performed all the tricks together. They took turns pulling rabbits out of hats; they took turns sawing each other in half.

My grandad died before I was born, and Gran stopped performing so much after that, though she kept up her love of magic. So she bought this little shop near the market, which is full of old furniture and clothes and books and curiosities from the past. And it's also stuffed full of magic stuff. Cards and tricks and coins and top hats and wands and silk handkerchiefs, and more.

The shop itself is narrow. I suppose the building used to be someone's terraced house back in Victorian times, and it's all still in the same shape: a front room, a back room, a long corridor lined with books and posters and dusty pictures and suits of armour and a stuffed crocodile.

Then there's a big room at the back where I think the old kitchen would have been, which is where Gran keeps the larger items, like wardrobes and chests and tables and boxes full of dusty treasure. There's an old milk pail, which Gran says Harry Houdini once used.

Harry Houdini was a super-famous

 89

escape artist, illusionist and stunt performer. Dad has a signed picture of him in his underwear, all wrapped in chains and about to jump into a river.

There's also a sequinned outfit on a tailor's dummy, which Gran says was worn by Debbie McGee, the beautiful assistant to the famous TV magician Paul Daniels.

There's even a coffin-thing with spikes on the inside that Gran says she used to use when she was onstage. She won't let me try it out, even though the spikes are fake and bend back when you close the lid.

Lucky came rushing up to me when I came in, and I knelt to give him a hug. I think he must have known I was a bit upset

because he gave me an extra-big lick. I
held out two fists. Lucky looked at them,
then lifted his paw and
tapped the one on the
right. I opened it to
reveal a Barkworth's
doggie treat.

'Every time!' I
said. 'How do you
know?'

Lucky winked at me, or so it seemed,
before he led me to the back, where Gran
was. She gave me a warm brownie and a
glass of milk, and I told her about my day.

'I wish I could do something about the
bullies,' I said. 'I wish I could summon up

a tornado and blow them into the Thames.
Or do a lightning spell to zap them. Or a
zombie curse to control their minds and
make them walk into the sea.'

'Dunno about all of that,' Gran said,
'but I can show you how to push a cup
through a table?'

'Thanks, Gran,' I said. 'But . . .'

'But what?' she asked.

'I love performing,' I said. 'But
sometimes I feel like it would be nice to
be able to do real magic, not just tricks. I
mean, what is a magician without magic?'

Gran sipped her tea thoughtfully, then
answered with, 'Ian?'

'Ha ha. Do you believe in magic, Gran?'

I asked, not letting it go. 'Real magic?'

Gran thought for a bit. 'I believe in you,' she said eventually. 'I believe in family and friends. And love. That's where the real magic is.'

'Those are all great, Gran,' I said. 'But that's not quite the same as being able to blast your enemies with a fireball.'

Just then the bell at the front of the shop rang and Gran had to go and serve a customer. It was after 6 p.m., but Gran was known for serving customers at all hours, though it's true that a lot of the time the 'customers' were just local folk popping in for a chinwag. Lucky and I chewed on our snacks, and I wandered

 93

around, looking at the old junk in the back room.

'Wait a sec, that's new,' I said, noticing something.

It was an old chest. Like a travelling steamer trunk or something, half hidden under a blanket. I slid the blanket away and saw letters printed across the top of the chest in faded gold ink. The letters read:

A.A. London.

And that was all.

'Mysterious,' I said.

Lucky came nosing across to peer over my shoulder. He was curious too.

Gran always had loads of old boxes and

chests and things in her shop. Often from
the house clearances of local people who'd
died. Everyone knew she was interested
in old things like this, and she'd get two
or three deliveries a month that she'd go
through between customers. She'd sell the
best stuff, give the decent stuff to charity
and take the rest to the tip. It took time
to work her way through everything, and
I'd sometimes help out. It was fun, though
sometimes sad, to go through people's
belongings: dusty books, cracked glasses
and pieces of bric-a-brac. Most of it was
junk, but there was the occasional treasure.

Maybe I'd find some treasure in this
chest! I certainly needed a bit of luck after

95

the day I'd had. I dropped to my knees and opened the lid.

Or I would have if it hadn't been locked.

Looking around, I couldn't see a key taped to the chest. But Max Magic doesn't need a key! I dug around in my coat pocket until I found my lock-pick, a special curved tool that you can use to open locks. An essential part of any magician's toolkit, it had been a present from Gran last Christmas. A lock-pick doesn't work on all locks, but I'd got pretty good at opening these old-fashioned ones. I felt around for the tumblers – the invisible wheels inside a lock – then used the saw part to push them all down. The lock clicked open.

'Doosh!' I whispered, feeling a surge of excitement.

I opened the lid. Then . . .

BAM!

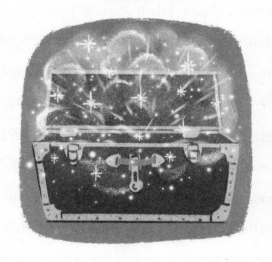

There was a bright flash of light, and I felt a thrilling shock run through my whole

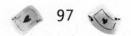

body, throwing me back against an old table, knocking the breath out of my lungs.

I sat there, blinking and shaking my head. Recovering from the shock.

What had just happened? I asked myself. Had there been a bomb in the trunk? Was it booby-trapped? But I didn't feel like I'd been blown up. In fact, I felt full of . . . power. Like there was energy crackling in my veins, concentrated in my chest. Maybe I'd had an electric shock?

A hazy wisp of smoke swirled lazily around the room, lit by the early evening sunbeams shining through the little windows of Gran's back room. My head swam, like I was in a different world.

'Well, that was weird!' a voice said.

Whose voice was that? Not mine. Not Gran's. But there was no one else here. Just . . .

Lucky.

I looked at the old dog.

Lucky looked back at me and said . . . 'Are there any more biscuits?'

5

Top That!

'What just happened?' I asked myself out loud.

'You opened that chest, there was a bang and a flash, you bumped your head and now you can understand what I'm saying,' Lucky replied. 'Now, about the biscuits . . .'

'Dogs can't talk,' I said, scrabbling backwards away from him in shock. 'I'm just imagining it.'

Lucky sat on his haunches and started scratching his ear with his hind leg. 'OK, you're the boss,' he said.

I crawled over to the open chest and looked inside. Inside the lid was an inscription. Someone's name and address.

Arthur Andrews

21 Limehouse Street

Spitalfields

London EC1

'Arthur Andrews,' I muttered. 'A.A.'
I felt inside the chest. It was dark and

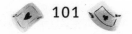

I couldn't quite see the contents, but I felt something round and hard. I pulled it out.

'A top hat,' I breathed in wonder.

It was class. Top quality. Dark blue velvety material over a stiff frame. Inside it was lined with some silky fabric, deep red in colour. It looked brand-new, like it had been made yesterday. But something told me it was old. At least as old as the chest.

I couldn't resist. I clapped it onto my head.

It fitted perfectly.

I felt a little thrill run through my body. Like the sensation I'd felt when I'd opened the lid of the chest, though much less shocking this time.

I peered inside the chest again. Underneath
where the hat had been lay a set of clothes,
neatly folded. I pulled them out. A dark
suit. Far too big for me. A grown-up's
suit, but fancy. Odd that the suit was for a
grown-up when the hat fitted a twelve-year-
old. But then again, nothing was making

much sense at the moment.

And that was that. There was nothing else in the chest.

'Nice hat!' Gran said, coming back into the room. 'Oh, you managed to get Mr Andrews's chest open.'

'Sorry, Gran,' I said, trying to act as normal as I could. I don't know why, but I didn't want to tell Gran what had just happened. She'd start asking questions I didn't have the answers to. 'I, er . . . shouldn't have been nosing around.'

'Oh, that's all right,' she said, laughing. 'I'd be more worried if a young boy didn't go poking around where he wasn't supposed to. Was the titfer in the chest?'

'Titfer?'

'Tit for tat: hat,' she explained. 'Rhyming slang.'

'Oh right, yes,' I said, laughing. 'There was a hat, and a suit. Who was Mr Andrews? Was he a magician too?'

'Not a magician,' Gran said, folding the suit and putting it back into the chest, 'but he was always curious about magic and mystery. A great traveller – he explored the world and made a lot of discoveries. He was always good to talk to, old Arthur.'

I took the hat off and handed it to her. She shook her head.

'You keep it,' she said. 'It's the first part of your stage outfit. One thing I know

is that if you find a hat that fits as well as that one, then it's yours forever.'

'Thanks, Gran,' I said.

I rubbed my head – I still felt slightly woozy from the bump.

'Are you OK?' Gran asked, looking at me curiously.

Sometimes she has this way of looking right into you, like she sees everything that's going on inside. For a moment I thought of telling her what had just happened. The bang and the flash and . . . the talking dog.

I looked at Lucky, who looked back at me with a sideways glance and whined inquisitively. I shook my head, which was

still feeling a bit cloudy. It had probably
been my imagination. Dogs can't talk! I just
needed to get outside and get some fresh
air. I grinned at Gran and popped the hat
back on my head.

'I'm absolutely fine,' I said.

But that wasn't true. I wasn't fine at all.

On the way home I began to feel very
strange indeed. Like that feeling you get
sometimes when you have a fever and the
room seems to tilt and the colours all seem
a bit off. I felt a bit dazed too. Maybe I
should have gone back to the shop to sit
down for a while, but it was getting dark and

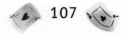

Mum would soon be expecting me home for tea.

'Max,' Lucky said as he trotted along beside me. 'Take a deep breath and pull yourself together.'

I groaned. He was still talking. So much for it being my imagination.

'I'm fine,' I hissed.

'You're not fine. You keep walking into walls and staring off into the distance,' he replied. 'People are looking at you strangely. Though I suppose that might be because of that stupid hat.'

'It's not stupid,' I muttered. I took a deep breath and continued on my unsteady way.

The walk home was punctuated with three Strange Events.

The first Strange Event happened as I passed a cafe on Aldgate. Still a bit unsteady on my pegs, I bumped into a table, knocking over a tall glass of milky  coffee. The man sitting at the table looked startled but didn't have time to react. Without even thinking about it, I quickly held out a hand. Something deep inside my chest tingled with energy and . . . the glass froze in mid-spill.

 109

The owner of the coffee had already started to cry out in annoyance but then he stopped, staring at the coffee cup, which was tilted, unmoving, in mid-air, great drops of frothy coffee also frozen in the act of sploshing out, like a paused TV show.

The man's mouth dropped open.

I twisted my hand slightly and the glass tilted back again!

The man and I watched the hot coffee slosh itself back into the glass. Not a drop was spilled.

'That is so cool,' Lucky said, his tail wagging in excitement.

The man stared at me in astonishment.

'Unbelievable,' he whispered.

I nodded. 'Tell me about it,' I said. Then I lowered my head and scurried off down the street. What was happening?

I was seeing things. That's what was happening. I must have hit my head harder than I'd thought. This was all in my imagination. I was dreaming. I was unconscious in a hospital bed with beeping machines and my loving family gathered around, weeping and clutching my hands. 'He's too young!' they'd be saying. 'Not Max the Magnificent, he can't die!'

Right?

'I'm hungry,' Lucky said loudly.

'Dogs can't talk,' I whispered, glancing

111

around nervously at the other pedestrians, though no one else seemed to have heard him.

'OK, sorry,' Lucky whispered back. 'But I am hungry.'

I turned to look at him. 'OK, so if you can talk, why didn't you talk in front of Gran?'

'She can't understand me,' Lucky said. He sat down and looked up at me, one ear up and one flopping down. 'She doesn't have magical powers like you. Or at least not exactly like you. I don't know why, but I can only talk to you. Everyone else just hears whining or barking.'

I shook my head. 'No. This is crazy.

None of this is happening.' I turned and
strode towards home, Lucky trotting along
behind me.

The second Strange Event happened as I
turned into Cobb Lane. I was
so distracted that I nearly
bumped into someone, a
lady in a business suit and
trainers, walking very fast
and looking at her phone.
We saw each other at the
last minute and I swerved
to avoid her. She glared
at me.

'Watch out, kid!' she
snapped.

 113

But no. Wait . . .

She hadn't **said** anything. 'Watch out, kid!' was what she had been thinking. What she'd **wanted** to say. But she'd held it in. I knew that as sure as I knew how to palm a coin. I turned and watched her stride off, still looking at her phone.

I had read her mind.

'No,' I muttered. 'Mind reading is . . . unbelievable.'

'As unbelievable as a talking dog,' Lucky agreed, sniffing around at the base of a red phone box.

It wasn't possible, I thought. I must have just guessed what she'd been thinking from the look on her face.

Right?

The third Strange Event was the strangest of all.

I decided it would be safer to take the bus for the last stretch. I don't usually take the bus, but I was still feeling distinctly wobbly and so when I saw the number 242 I decided to hop on. Lucky followed, sighing. He was fine on buses, although, like me, he preferred to walk.

I reached into the pocket I always keep my travel card in, but my fingers closed over nothing.

The driver tapped the screen between us impatiently as I just stood there.

I closed my eyes, trying to visualise

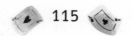 115

where I'd left my travel card. There it was. On my desk at home. I could see it in my mind's eye.

The driver tapped again and I pulled my hand out of my pocket, ready to say sorry and get back off the bus.

Then I looked at my hand.

The travel card was there, between my fingers. My eyes bulged. My heart raced. My breath caught in my chest. My fingers had been empty just seconds before! Where had this card come from? 'How did you do that, Max?' Lucky asked. 'You closed your eyes and the card just appeared.'

Then the bus lurched and I grabbed a seat, Lucky settling down beside me. I looked down, but the card had gone. My hand was empty again.

'An illusion,' Lucky whispered. 'That is so, so cool.' His tail wagged again.

That one was harder to explain away. I could convince myself that I might have imagined it. But the driver had seen it too. And believe me, London bus drivers are not easy people to fool.

I hopped off the bus at our stop and went in via the back garden. We don't tend to use the front door much. Vinny

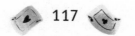

was there as usual in the gloom, kicking
his football against the garden wall. He'd
be out here until it was pitch black or Mum
yelled at him to stop the noise! Thud, thud,
thud. I'm convinced that one day the whole
wall will come crashing down and we'll
be face to face with the Singh family next
door.

Vinny saw me and volleyed the ball
towards me.

'Head it!' he called with a grin.

But I'd already bashed my head once
today and I didn't want to do any more
damage. I lifted a hand to protect myself,
brushed the ball with my little finger
and . . .

Doosh!

The ball pinged off my finger and shot directly upwards like it had been fired from a cannon. I had hardly even touched it.

My brother and I looked up in amazement as the ball disappeared into the darkening sky, still rising until it was lost in the gloom.

'Huh . . . huh . . . handball,' he said quietly.

'Come on, Lucky,' I said, rushing into the house before Vinny could say anything else.

Susie was at the kitchen table, chatting to one of her friends on the phone. As I passed her, she let out a little cry of annoyance.

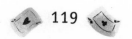 119

'My phone just turned itself off,' she complained.

'Praise the stars!' Mum said, winking at me. 'Half a minute's peace.'

I grinned weakly and headed for the stairs.

Had I turned Susie's phone off? And what had happened with Vinny's football?

I stopped and turned back to Mum. 'Is Dad home?' I asked, wondering if she knew about the incident with the stall and the Crayfish Twins.

She shook her head. 'No, he texted to say he was going to be a bit late.'

I wondered if I should tell her what had happened, but decided I'd leave it to Dad.

My head was spinning with all today's craziness, and I just needed to get up to my room and collect my thoughts. I turned to go.

Mum called out after me and I stopped again, in the doorway.

'So, was the horoscope right?' she asked.

'H-horoscope?' I replied, confused.

'This morning, remember? Today was supposed to be a day of destiny for you. Anything magical happen today?'

'Um . . .' I said, then hesitated. Mum is always there when I need her, but I didn't see how she could help me with this. Besides, she and Dad had other problems

 121

on their plate, what with the bills and the
Crayfish Twins.

I shook my head. 'No, nothing like that,'
I said.

I mean, how could I even start to explain
what was happening to me? She wouldn't
believe it anyway. She'd just blame it on the
bump on the head and she'd start on about
concussion and want to take me down to
A & E. Mums are like that. Always dragging
you off to A & E for the tiniest thing.

'Oh, you bumped your head: A & E!
Oh, you have a temperature: A & E. Ooh,
you pulled the dresser over onto yourself
while performing a magic trick: off to
A & E we go!'

Chris walked in and stopped dead, looking at the wall.

'That flipping clock is broken again,' he said. 'The hands are going backwards!'

I looked at the clock. He was right. Was I doing this? Was I shooting off some weird . . . I don't know . . . electricity?

'Is something wrong, Max?' Mum asked, as she saw the look on my face.

Susie was watching me too. 'You look weird,' she said. 'Even weirder than usual. And I don't just mean that stupid hat.'

'Everything's fine. And it's not stupid,' I said, forcing a smile. 'I'm going up to my room. Got some homework to do.'

'Now I know something's wrong,' Mum

x

123

said. 'You doing homework without me standing over you?'

I laughed nervously.

'Go on then,' she said. 'Dinner will be ready in twenty minutes. I'll give you a yell.'

For once, though, I didn't feel hungry, but I forced a grin, turned and ran up the stairs to my room, Lucky following.

I shut the door behind us and leaned against it, my heart thumping, head racing. My eyes flicked over to my desk. Sure enough, my travel card was lying there, just as I'd pictured it.

There was a loud bang outside.

Then someone cried out, 'Nooooooo!'

'What was that?' I asked.

'That was Vinny's football finally coming down,' Lucky said, peering out the window. 'It kind of exploded.'

He jumped up on the bed, turned to face me and sat on his haunches. 'Are you OK, Max?' he asked. 'You're looking kind of pale.'

'No, I'm not OK,' I replied. 'I'm talking to a dog!'

'You probably need to eat some dog food,' Lucky said. 'Whenever I feel bad I eat some dog food and then I feel better.'

'That's it?' I said. 'That's your advice? Eat dog food?'

'Sorry, that's all I've got,' Lucky said,

scratching himself. 'I may be able to talk, but I am still a dog after all. Maybe you need to talk to your human family about this.'

'Not yet,' I said. 'I need to think. Maybe I'll wake up tomorrow and everything will have gone back to normal.'

'If that's the case,' Lucky said, 'then please try to remember that I told you I don't like the Woofman's dog food so much. I prefer Waggy Boy.'

'W-what?' I asked.

'Well, if you wake up tomorrow and I've stopped talking, I won't get another chance to tell you,' he said. 'So maybe write it down? Waggy Boy, especially the beef. But sometimes chicken makes a nice change. And turkey at Christmas, obviously.'

I took a deep breath, trying to calm down.

'Maybe it's the hat,' I muttered. 'Maybe this . . . power is in the hat.'

Lucky cocked his head doubtfully.

 127

'You weren't wearing the hat when you started to understand what I was saying,' he pointed out.

Nevertheless, I took the hat and tossed it onto an armchair across the room. Then I looked around for a way to test my theory about the power being in the hat.

There was a half-full glass of water on the little cabinet next to my bed. Remembering the incident with the coffee, I held out a hand towards the glass and concentrated. I felt the tingle from my chest spreading out down my arm to my fingertips. The glass trembled. I breathed in. Could I do this? Could I really control objects? I twisted my hand ever so slightly.

The glass flung itself off the nightstand, spraying water everywhere and smashing on the thin carpet.

'I don't think it's the hat,' Lucky said.

'Did I do that?' I asked the old dog. 'Did I control that glass?'

'If control means drench the curtains and smash the glass on the floor, then yes,' Lucky replied. 'You controlled the heck out of it.'

Mum called us down for tea. I put the hat back on. It felt comfortable on me, and had the added bonus of hiding the bruise on my bonce.

'FOOD!' Lucky barked, jumping down onto the floor and spinning in a tight circle.

'Hope it's Waggy Boy. Come on, Max.'

I got up and went over to the door. But I paused before opening it. My hand was shaking. My heart was pounding. In fact I was scared. Really scared.

'Is this real, Lucky?' I asked, looking down at him, my voice shaking. 'Is this real . . . magic?'

'I think so,' he replied. 'Isn't that what you wanted?'

When I got downstairs, Dad was back. He was stacking the dishwasher and talking to Mum in a quiet voice. He looked worried, and she looked a bit shocked. I guess he'd just told her about the Crayfish Twins. My heart sank further.

Then Dad spotted me and gave me a big smile.

'All right, love?' Mum said, turning and putting her own bright smile on. 'Come and sit down. I'll get you a plate.' I guessed they were trying to protect me from their money worries.

I really wasn't hungry but I sat and said, 'Thanks, Mum, I'm starving.' If I didn't say that, she'd definitely know something was wrong.

The others were chatting away at the dinner table. Susie was texting as she talked. Vinny was pumping up a new football, fresh out of the wrapper. Chris was inspecting the insides of the clock.

Lucky was groaning with delight as he scoffed his food.

'Waggy Boy!' he said through a mouthful of beef. 'So good.'

'What's he growling about?' Dad muttered to no one in particular as he set the dishwasher running.

'I saw that bloke off the telly on the bus today,' Susie said.

'Which one?' Vinny asked.

'The number 38,' Susie replied. 'Towards Clapton Pond.'

'Take your hat off for dinner, Max,' Mum said as she turned and saw me.

'Where did you get that hat anyway?' Vinny asked. 'It's certainly . . . unusual.'

I took it off and inspected it.

'It's definitely a hat that might divide opinion,' Mum said politely.

'Yeah, on the one hand, there are those that think it looks ridiculous,' Susie said, 'and on the other hand, there's Max.'

Everyone laughed at this, including Lucky. I shot him a look of betrayal.

'Now, now,' Mum said. 'Don't tease Max, please. And stop barking, Lucky! Chris, put that clock away!'

I still didn't have much appetite. But I tried to eat something so the others wouldn't get too suspicious. But even if they had suspected something was up, they wouldn't have had a chance to interrogate

me, because there were more Strange Events throughout the meal. The lights kept going off and on, the television kept switching itself to a weather channel from Toronto and, as Dad was serving up the pudding, the dishwasher door pinged open and showered us with soapy water. Dad ran off to grab a mop.

'Must be some sort of electrical interference,' Chris said, jumping up to inspect the fuse box, suds dripping from his nose. 'Like there's something in the house randomly firing energy around.'

I didn't tell him the something was me, and as the meal went on I tried my best to see if I could control it. I found that if I took deep breaths, relaxed and tried to empty my mind, the Strange Events seemed to calm down. And by the end of the meal I thought maybe I was getting the hang of it.

After dinner, as Chris was pulling the dishwasher apart, looking puzzled, I made my excuses and went up to my room again. I lay on the bed and tried to calm the tingling in my chest, the buzzing in my head and the churning in my tummy.

Lucky lay beside me.

'Max?' he said.

I jumped. I still hadn't got used to the idea of a talking dog.

'Yes?' I replied.

'When you're a famous magician, can I be your onstage assistant?'

'A dog as an assistant?' I said.

'Yeah, you can call me your Labracadabrador.'

'But you're not a Labrador,' I said. 'You're a terrier.'

'Can't a dog dream?' he said.

'I dunno what's going to happen,' I said after I'd stopped laughing, Lucky always made me feel better. And weirdly, I was getting used to him talking. In a way, I think I'd always been able to understand him.

'But one thing is for sure,' I went on. 'If this is going to be a permanent . . .

change in me, then I need to figure out how to control this power. At the moment, I can't even control a glass of water.'

I lay there, thinking things over. I wasn't sure I could do this on my own. I needed help. I needed advice. And not just doggie advice.

I needed my friends.

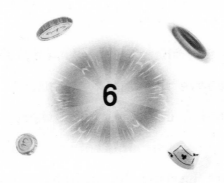

6

Shelf Hazard

The book slowly rose from the floor and spun in mid-air. I was concentrating really hard on not letting it fly off and bonk someone on the head.

'Holy moly,' Stretch said.

'Awesome,' Daisy said.

'I can see the string,' Sophie said.

'There are no strings,' I said, swiping my hand above the book.

'OK, then I can see the mirror,' Sophie said.

'It's not mirrors,' I sighed.

'It's always mirrors,' Sophie said. 'If it's not strings.'

We had arranged to meet up in the library at lunchtime. I wasn't much of a reader, to be honest, but Bottley was even less of a reader, so I figured we'd be pretty safe from him in here. Also, I needed somewhere quiet to demonstrate my new powers to my friends. Only Sophie didn't seem convinced.

'Look, I'm telling you, it's magic,' I

139

said. 'Real magic. I opened the chest and there was a light, and a flash and . . . well, this all started happening. There was something in that chest, left by Arthur Anderson maybe. Something he brought back from his travels. Some power, some force, some spirit.'

'Some mirrors,' Sophie said, folding her arms.

I let the book drop with a slam onto the floor. I felt cross. After all, it had been a stressful twenty-four hours.

'It's **magic**, Sophie. **Real** magic.'

'Shhhh,' someone behind me said. 'Don't you know this is a library, Mullers?'

With a sinking feeling, I turned around.

Bottley had found us.

Bottley, in a library? It was like seeing a hippo in a helicopter, a rhino in a racing car, a gorilla in a . . . Well, a gorilla in a library.

 141

Everyone groaned.

'All I want is to be included,' Bottley said, with a look of fake sadness on his face.

'Oh, leave us alone,' Stretch said. He stood up and stepped towards Bottley, who, without even taking his eyes off me, reached out and shoved Stretch back down onto the floor.

'Now,' Bottley said to me, 'since you're so good at magic, how about you have a little look behind my ear and see if you can find anything?'

'Fleas?' Sophie suggested.

'Dandruff?' Stretch said.

'A worm?' Daisy said.

Bottley ignored them, grabbed the front of my shirt and hauled me up, bringing my face so close to his that I could see the straggly, tufty bits of hair sprouting from his chin. 'And just so we're clear, I haven't forgotten the incident with the egg, you little squirt,' he growled.

Suddenly it was all too much.

The egg incident, the Crayfish Twins, the bang on the head, the argument with Sophie, and now this.

I felt a powerful tingling in my chest again. I reached out, as if to push Bottley away, and then it happened.

Boom! Flash!

Bottley went flying away from me like I'd hit him with Thor's hammer.

He let out a little whimper as he flew, then slammed into a shelf full of textbooks and slumped to the floor, looking shocked. A book fell down from the top shelf, bounced off his head and fell open in his lap to reveal a full double-page spread about gorillas.

The whole set of shelves tottered, leaned . . .

. . . and fell over, away from us.

Crash!

The bookshelf toppled into the one next to it, which also went over, crashing into

the next and knocking that over too. One
by one the library shelves went down like
dominoes.

Students screamed and scurried out of
the way while I was frozen to the spot,
watching in horror. But there was another
feeling in there too. Excitement.

I felt someone plucking at my sleeve. It
was Daisy.

'I think we'd better leg it,' she said.

'Still think it was mirrors, Sophie?' Stretch
asked, once we had taken refuge on the far
side of the football pitch.

'No,' she said thoughtfully. 'I don't

think that was mirrors.'

'This is amazing, Max,' Daisy said, striding around in great excitement. 'You can do magic. Genuine, real magic!'

'But I can't control it,' I said.

My heart was pounding and my stomach churning, but underneath it all was still that little feeling of excitement.

'What else can you do, Max?' Stretch asked. 'You reckon you could make yourself invisible?'

'I thought about that but I really can't see myself doing it,' I said, with a little wink.

'This is no time for jokes,' Sophie said. 'You could have really hurt Bottley back

there.' She wasn't annoyed at me. She
seemed worried.

'Or even worse, you could have hurt
someone you like,' said Stretch.

'Yeah,' Daisy said, chuckling. 'And
let's face it, Bottley only had his-SHELF to
blame.'

Sophie shot them a cross look, then
turned back to me.

'What's happening, Soph?' I asked.
'You're the smart one.'

She shook her head. 'I don't know,
Max,' she said. 'I promise you we'll figure
this out. The most important thing is to
get it under control. Before someone gets
seriously hurt.'

'Yeah, I know,' I said, my shoulders slumping. Sophie was right. That little flash of excitement I'd felt in the library when I'd zapped Bottley – that wasn't good.

'Do you think you could control it if you practised?' she asked. 'You're always saying that practice is the key.'

I looked up at her. She was right. Magic is all about practice. Practice, practice and more practice.

'I can learn to control this,' I said firmly.

'Good,' Sophie said. 'And just think, Max. If you can learn to control your powers . . . ?' She raised an eyebrow.

I looked up at her and grinned. She was right again. If I learned to control my powers, well, what couldn't I achieve? I really could be Max the Magnificent.

'OK,' Sophie said. She took out the little notebook she carries everywhere with her. She calls it her Business Book, though if you ask her why she calls it that she says it's none of your business.

She started scribbling in the book. 'I'm going to put together a timetable and we'll start after school, in the churchyard near the market.'

'Start what?' I asked.

'Your magical training,' she replied.

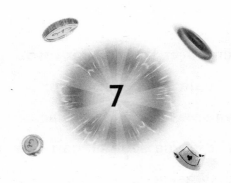

7

Learning Lessons

'OK,' Sophie said, reading from her Business Book. 'So it seems like you have three types of magical power: telekinesis, mind reading and illusions.'

We were on the way to the churchyard after school and I'd been filling them in on all the Strange Events of the night before.

'Oh, and I can talk to dogs now,' I said.

Everyone was silent for a bit.

'Sorry, did you say you can talk to dogs?' Daisy asked.

'Yeah. Well, I can talk to Lucky at least, and he can talk to me.'

There was another silence.

Then Sophie shook her head. 'OK, that's just too weird to deal with right now. We'll come back to that.'

'Do you really know what you're doing, Sophie?' Daisy asked.

'I've drawn up lesson plans, study aids and a mind-map,' Sophie said, waving her notebook.

'This is magic,' Stretch said. 'Not design tech.'

'Same principle,' Sophie said. 'Look, whatever you're doing, whether it's magic, design tech, maths, or, I don't know, learning to tie your shoelaces, a learning plan is essential.'

Stretch and Daisy exchanged a doubtful look.

'Today we're going to work on telekinesis,' Sophie said.

'My dad got telekinesis,' Daisy said. 'His throat swelled up so much he couldn't talk. Mum was quite pleased.'

'That's tonsilitis,' Sophie said. 'Telekinesis is something different.'

'I think Telekinesis plays for Arsenal,' Stretch said. 'On loan from Athens.'

'Telekinesis is the power of moving things with your mind,' Sophie explained patiently. She walked over to a low wall on the other side of the churchyard and placed a soft-drink can she'd found in a bin on top of it. 'See if you can knock this over.'

I took a deep breath and concentrated. I felt the tingling in my chest again, but maybe this time it wasn't so scary. Was I getting used to it? I held out my hand and pointed a finger at the can.

DOOSH!

I felt a surge run down my arm and

153

shoot out of my finger, firing off towards
the can.

Crunch!

The wall shuddered under the impact
and a brick fell out. The can, though,
didn't move. I'd missed.

'Again!' Sophie cried.

I took another breath and fired again.

Once more I missed the can and hit the
wall instead, sending chips of brickwork
and pieces of moss flying.

'I can hit it with a stone if you like,'
Stretch said helpfully.

'Again!' Sophie yelled, ignoring him.

For a third time I pointed, concentrated

and fired. This time
I hit the can.

With a loud clang,
it shot off at an
angle, hurtled
across the churchyard and
smashed right through a toilet window at the
back of the church. Someone inside yelled,
'Oi!' and the furious face of the church
warden appeared through the broken pane.

'I think you're getting the hang of it,'
Stretch said, admiration in his voice.

'LEG IT!' Daisy cried, and once again we
found ourselves running from trouble.

As we raced away, the feeling of power
coursing through my body made me giddy.

 155

I let out a laugh and turned at the gate
to the churchyard to see if we were being
chased. My laugh was cut short when I
spotted a head peeping up from behind a
gravestone. Someone who'd been spying on
us. Someone wearing a yellow coat.

Bottley.

When we felt we were safely away from
the warden and Bottley, Stretch and I said
goodbye to the others. Stretch's parents also
have a stall in the market, selling china tea
sets, plates, teapots, cups, you name it, so
we were heading in the same direction.

'I think it might be sensible to try and

keep your powers . . . under wraps,'
Sophie said as we were about to part.

'What do you mean?'

'Well, do you really want to draw
attention to yourself?' she asked.

I shrugged. 'Have you met me?' I
asked. 'I always want to draw attention
to myself.'

'If people find out you can do real
magic,' she said, 'well, it might attract the
wrong sort of attention, from the wrong
sort of people.'

'Like who?'

'Like those criminal twins, or bullies, or
. . . I don't know, the government. They
might cart you off and do tests on you.'

 157

'Does this mean I have to lose the hat?' I asked.

'It's not just the hat,' Sophie said. 'It's all the magic stuff too.'

I grinned. 'Don't worry,' I said. 'I can look after myself.'

'Just keep a low profile, OK?' she said.

We walked along, Stretch chattering away nineteen to the dozen, talking about Bottley and why he might have been spying on us.

'I hate bullies,' he was saying. 'Every time I see Bottley, I get the fight or flight instinct. Why is it only fight or flight? There should be a third option.'

'There is,' I said absently. 'It's called dying.'

I wasn't paying much attention though. I was thinking about telekinesis, and how I could use it, onstage and off.

We turned into Wentworth Street and the first thing I saw was a businessman in a fancy suit. There are a lot of businesspeople around this area. We're very close to the City of London, which is full of banks and law firms and other places that employ people who wear suits and earn loads of money.

And speaking of money, I could see the businessman's fat wallet half hanging out of his back pocket. He was booming into his mobile phone as he stood in front of a posh restaurant.

'Sell, sell, sell,' the man said confidently, just as we approached. 'New York won't like it, but we'll make millions!'

As I passed him, almost without thinking about it, I twitched my finger and the man's wallet popped out of his pocket and fell. Without breaking my stride, I snatched it out of the air, carried on and turned into Old Street. Once we'd turned the corner I stopped and opened the wallet. It was stuffed full of fifty-pound notes! I was rich! I could pay off the Crayfish

Twins and still have money left over. I could buy the cloak I'd had my eye on for my stage costume. I could buy a wand, a brand-new set of magic tricks. I could buy a dove. Or a rabbit!

Then I caught Stretch's eye. My friend was watching me with an odd expression on his face.

'What?' I asked. Though I knew.

'Is this why you wanted to find real magic?' he asked quietly. 'So you could steal wallets?'

'But, Stretch! This would solve all of my problems,' I said, holding up the wallet. 'Can't I just keep this? That businessman didn't sound very nice.

 161

Isn't what he does just as bad?'

'It doesn't matter what other people do,' Stretch said gently. 'It only matters what **you** do. It's the same with Bottley. Just because he's a bully, it doesn't make it OK for you to be one too.'

I sighed. 'OK,' I said. 'I'm sorry, Stretch. You're right.'

'Great,' Stretch said. Then he stood and watched me.

I watched him right back.

'So . . . ?' he said.

'So . . . what?'

'Aren't you going to take the wallet back?'

'Yes, OK.' I trotted back around the

corner, ran up to the businessman and
tapped him on the shoulder.

He turned with a grumpy look on his face
and I handed him his wallet.

'Oh,' the man said, surprised. 'Thank
you.'

'No problem,' I said. 'You know, you
should really keep that in your inside jacket
pocket. Next to your heart.'

'Yes,' the man said, doing just that.

'After all,' I went on, 'you don't know
who's about.'

When I got home that evening after stopping
in at Gran's, Dad and Mum were talking in

the kitchen. I don't know what made me do it, but I stopped just outside the back door and listened. I know eavesdropping is wrong, but there was something about my dad's voice that got me worried.

'I dunno what we're going to do, Molly,' he said. 'These Crayfish boys are going to get us shut down.'

'Is there no way we can find the £250?' Mum asked.

'I've just spent everything I have on more stock,' Dad said. 'I've got nothing left.'

'I could take on some more shifts at the hospital,' Mum said.

'You already work too hard, Molly,'

Dad said. 'Anyway, it won't stop at the £250. They were around again today, said they'll be wanting more money for "insurance", as they call it. They're robbing me blind.'

'What about the police?' Mum asked.

'They're worse than useless,' Dad said. 'That PC Peaceful doesn't do a thing. All he's worried about is keeping things quiet. And the Crayfish Twins are too careful to do anything right under his nose.'

'So what's the answer?' Mum asked. 'You can't sell the stall. Not Mullers' Toys!'

I gasped at hearing this and clamped a hand over my mouth.

'I don't know if we've got an

165

alternative,' Dad said. 'If I can't find a way to magic up £250 in two days, then it's all over.'

Just then, Lucky barked.

I glared at him and he shrugged.

'I'm hungry,' he explained.

'Max?' I heard Mum call. I groaned inwardly and pushed the door open. I had to show myself. Mum and Dad gave each other a little glance as I came in.

'All right, love?' Mum said. 'Good day at school?'

'It was fine, Mum, yeah,' I said. It had been a good day for the most part, I thought.

Weird. Strange. Magical. Unbelievable.

But right now all I could think of was what Dad had said, and the worried tone I'd heard in his voice. Then the dishwasher door pinged open again and showered us all with dishwater.

I had a restless night's sleep, dreaming of bullies chasing me and Lucky around the rim of a gigantic top hat while Chris sprayed soapy dishwater at us, Vinny kicked footballs at my head and Susie kept sending me distracting text messages. Then I woke up and immediately started worrying again.

Dad wouldn't lose the stall, would he? If he did, it would be because of me.

Because of what I'd let Bottley do with the boomerangs.

Then I had another thought. Was this why I had been given my gift? So I could fight back against the Crayfish Twins? And against Bottley? And against all the other bullies in this world?

I had wished that I could blast them with a fireball, after all.

Now I actually had the power.

Then I remembered the look Stretch had given me when I took the businessman's wallet.

But that was different. Stealing was wrong. Taking down bullies, on the other hand . . .

I tossed and turned so much Lucky got cross with me.

'I'm sleeping on the sofa,' he grumbled, and headed downstairs.

Great, I thought. Even my dog doesn't want to be around me.

Next morning it was pretty clear that Mum realised something was wrong. And not just because I had got up so early.

'What's on your mind, Max?' she asked as I was packing my school bag.

'Nothing, Mum,' I said, forcing myself to smile. 'What's my horoscope say?'

She grinned and grabbed the paper.

'It says today you will make a big decision.'
She winked at me and read on. 'It says you
must seize the day.' She bopped me on the
head with the rolled-up newspaper. 'Go do
some seizing, Max Magic.'

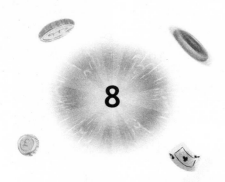

8

Mind-Reading Mayhem

Usually Mum drops Lucky at Gran's in the morning but today I decided I wanted to walk with him. It was nice to have someone to chat with, even if most of the conversation was Lucky asking endless questions like, which were more annoying – squirrels or cats? Or who would win a race

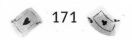

between a fox and a wolf? Or did I really think Barkworth's Doggy Treats were 100 per cent beef?

It was actually a welcome relief from worrying about the Crayfish Twins.

I dropped Lucky at Gran's and reluctantly decided to leave the top hat there as well. I loved the hat, but it did tend to attract a lot of attention, and Sophie had told me to keep a low profile. It was still early when I set off to school, but I'd messaged ahead and the gang were all ready and waiting. We'd decided we needed to avoid the church for a while, at least until the window got fixed. So we'd agreed to meet on the far side of the football field, where you're hidden from the school buildings by some trees.

'What's today's lesson?' I asked.

'Telepathy,' Sophie said.

'Is that when you can't be bothered to do something?' Daisy asked.

'That's apathy,' Sophie explained patiently.

'Yeah, Daisy,' Stretch said. 'Telepathy is when you understand what someone else is going through.'

'That's empathy,' Sophie said. 'TEL-EP-ATHY is being able to read someone's mind, or talk to them without speaking, by using your mind.'

 173

Daisy and Stretch nodded firmly, as if they understood.

'Now, I'm going to think of an object, Max,' Sophie said, 'and you need to concentrate and try to tell me what I'm thinking.'

'OK,' I said, frowning and looking her in the eye. I concentrated hard.

'Is it a book?' I asked after a moment.

She blinked and looked surprised. Then she nodded. 'It is a book!' she exclaimed.

'That doesn't prove anything,' Stretch muttered. 'Books is all she ever thinks about.'

'I've got one,' Daring Daisy cried, delighted. 'Do me!'

I turned to look at her and thought hard. 'Mount Everest,' I said.

Daisy gasped. 'I am!' she said. 'I am going to climb Mount Everest one day. I'm going to be the first girl to climb Mount Everest and then come back down on a zip wire.'

'Read my mind!' Stretch said.

'OK,' I replied, and watched his face intently. But after a few seconds I just wasn't getting anything. 'I can't tell what you're thinking about,' I said.

'Oh, am I supposed to be thinking about something?' Stretch asked. 'Sorry, try again.'

Instantly an image popped into my head.

 175

Sharp as anything.

'Teapot,' I said.

'Ooh, I could murder a cup of tea,' Stretch said.

'DOOSH!' I cried, delighted.

'Well,' Sophie said, ticking something off in her Business Book, 'you seem to have mind reading under control at least. Let's meet back here after school and we'll work on the third power. The power of illusion!'

I wasn't keen on the idea of having to wait until after school to carry on practising my magic, but it turned out I didn't have to. The telepathy came in handy during our history quiz.

Every time Mrs Jolopara asked me a question, I just had a quick look inside her brain and there the answer was.

'When was the Great Fire of London?'

'1666.'

'Who was Henry VIII's third wife?'

'Jane Seymour.'

'Who was the fortieth President of the United States?'

'Ronald Reagan.'

She stared at me in astonishment.

A few other students were also looking at me, as I never normally got questions right. Sophie was at the front of the class, eyeing me sternly. But I was enjoying myself too much to stop now.

 177

'I'll have to make these harder, Mr Mullers,' Mrs Jolopara said. 'What was Winston Churchill's middle name?'

'Trick question,' I answered straight away. 'He had two middle names. Sir Winston Leonard Spencer Churchill.'

Now the **entire** class was staring at me. Sophie was at the front, slowly shaking her head, warning me.

I swallowed nervously. Better get the next one wrong, I thought.

'What illness did King George III suffer from?'

I could see the answer at the front of her mind. It was something called porphyria, which I'd actually thought was

 179

a type of dolphin. If I guessed right, then everyone would know there was something up.

'Uncontrollable farting,' I said, and everyone laughed.

Mrs Jolopara looked at me for a moment longer before she moved on. The eyes of my classmates swivelled around again.

The show was over. Danger averted.

I grinned.

Then I saw Bottley, who was still staring at me. Staring right into my eyes. He knew something was up.

I swallowed nervously and looked down at the book in front of me.

After school we met up again by the
football pitch.

Sophie wagged a finger at me. 'What
were you playing at there in history?' she
asked. 'I thought you were going to try and
keep this a secret.'

'Sorry,' I said. 'I got carried away.'

'Learning to control your powers doesn't
just mean controlling the magic,' Sophie
lectured me. 'You have to learn to control
yourself too.'

I frowned. 'That's easy for you to say,'
I told her. 'You always know the right
answer. I always get everything wrong.

 181

You don't know what it's like to be the class dummy.'

She stared at me. 'You're not the class dummy,' she said.

'No,' Daisy said. 'That's Stretch.'

'No one's a dummy!' Sophie snapped.

'Well, no. Not any more,' I said. 'Not now I have the magic.'

'You didn't need the magic,' Sophie said. 'You were never a dummy. You just didn't . . . apply yourself as hard as you could.'

I didn't say anything. I was annoyed she was right.

'But that's all going to change now, isn't it?' she asked.

I nodded.

'So it's time for your next lesson,'
Sophie said. 'Go on, do an illusion.'

'Not "an illusion",' I said, still
feeling a bit sullen. 'You have to say
an illoo-OOO-oosion.'

'An illusion,' Sophie replied, flatly.

'No, you have to say illoo-OOO-oosion,'
I repeated. 'In a spooky voice. It's all
part of the theatre of the mind.'

'OK.' Sophie sighed. 'Show us your
illoo-OOOOOOOOOOOOO-oosion then.'

'Fine,' I said. I closed my eyes, held
my breath and concentrated.

I knew exactly what I was going to
create, and it was clear as day in my
mind's eye. I had to visualise it, just like

I'd visualised the travel card.

I heard a gasp from Daisy.

'Oh my goodness,' Sophie said.

'Holy roly moly,' Stretch added.

I opened my eyes. A hole had opened in the earth between us, and out of it had risen a huge snake. Red and black, with yellow glowing eyes. It looked at each of us in turn, hissing and spitting.

It looked real, it looked terrifying, it looked **hungry**.

The snake lunged forward, snapping at Stretch, who shrieked in alarm and did a back flip to escape. The creature darted towards Daisy, who ducked under it. Just like Daring Daisy to hold her ground, I thought with a grin. Then the snake turned to Sophie.

'OK, OK,' she said quickly. 'I think we've probably seen enough illoo-OOO-oosions for now, Max.'

I grinned, snapped my fingers, and the snake disappeared. And as it did, I saw a hint of movement in the trees. Could it have been a flash of yellow coat?

Stretch was breathing hard, his eyes wide with shock. 'I don't believe what I just saw,' he said.

'It was an illusion,' Sophie said. 'It wasn't real.'

'It looked real,' Daisy said. 'I felt its breath on my skin.'

'It was a very good illusion, I'll give you that,' Sophie said with a shiver. 'Max, promise me you won't go around scaring people like that again. That was just too real.'

'I do think I'm starting to get the hang of things,' I said, peering across the football pitch, looking for Bottley. 'Maybe it's time to seize the day.'

'What do you mean?' Sophie said.

Daisy and Stretch exchanged a slightly worried look, but before I could explain

myself I saw the flash of yellow again. This
time there was no doubt. It was Bottley,
running away across the football pitch. He
must have seen what we were up to.

I turned back to my friends, my mind
made up. I'd had enough of worrying about
what Bottley's next move would be. 'Seize
the day,' I said confidently. 'I mean, maybe
there are some people in this town who
need to get a taste of their own medicine.'

Feeling pretty pleased with myself, I
marched straight to the market, not even
bothering to keep an eye out for Bottley.
Mr Kumar saw me and frisbeed me my

 187

poppadom, which I snatched out of the air with a thanks. I laughed out loud as I marched down Petticoat Lane, munching on my poppadom, head held high. Just last night I'd been feeling scared and miserable. I had had so many worries on my back. But now everything was going to be . . . well, magic!

I was Max the Magnificent! I was going to deal with Bottley. Then I was going to deal with the Crayfish Twins and save the family business.

Everything went really well on the stall too. Dad had asked me to focus on selling wooden blocks for babies as we had a lot of stock and they weren't shifting. Maybe

Sophie was right when she said I shouldn't draw attention to myself. But if I was going to seize the day, then surely a little bit of magic wouldn't hurt?

I used my powers of telekinesis to help me stack the wooden blocks into a huge tower. It swayed back and forth in the breeze, looking like it was going to topple over, but I kept it upright with an occasional little flick of my magic finger. A big crowd gathered to watch me build it, and I made loads of sales.

Dad was so pleased with me. I watched him put the cash I'd earned in with the day's takings and count the lot.

'How much is it, Dad?' I asked. 'Is it

enough to pay off the Crayfish Twins?'

He smiled and ruffled my hair. 'Not quite, Max, but you've done a great job. It's a really good start. I'm so proud of you.'

I was pretty proud of me too, to be honest. As I went to see Gran and get Lucky, I sat chewing on a delicious muffin and chattering away with my mouth full about what a great day I'd had and how many blocks I'd sold and how I was going to invent loads of brilliant stage tricks and get one into the Magic Hall of Fame in Paris one day.

'I'm going to be the best magician there ever was, Gran,' I said.

She nodded.

'Everyone's going to come and see Max the Magnificent,' I went on, 'the Most Powerful Magician in the World!'

'You have a gift, all right,' Gran said quietly. 'A very special gift.'

I looked at her and shifted uncomfortably in my seat. Did she know? Had I let my secret out? Maybe it was time to tell her everything. She might tell Mum and Dad though. I hesitated.

'But a gift can be a burden as well,' she went on. 'The hardest lesson of all to learn is not **how** to use your gifts, but when not to use them at all.'

'What does that mean?' I asked.

She leaned across and put her hand

191

on my chest. Right where I could feel the magic tingle. Could she feel it too?

'The real power comes from here,' she said.

'I know,' I replied, nodding. 'That's where my magic comes from. My chest.'

'I mean from your horse,' she said.

'Horse?'

'Horse and cart: heart!' she explained. 'And it's not really magic I'm talking about. It's the power of friendship, and of family, and of love.'

I swallowed but didn't say anything. It was time to listen. I could see Lucky out the corner of my eye. He was listening too. He hadn't even finished his muffin.

'If you forget those things,' Gran went on softly, 'then all the magic in the world won't do you no good. Do you understand?'

I nodded. I thought I did.

'Gran,' I said, 'the other day, when I opened that old wooden chest . . .'

But then the bell tinkled at the front of the shop and she stood up to go and see to her customer. Before she went, she took the hat from where I'd left it that morning and plopped it back on my head with a wink. The moment was gone.

I was lost in thought as I walked home with Lucky that night. The old dog was chatting away about muffins and bones and interesting smells he'd noticed on the street.

'Ooh, Miffy has been here today,' he said
as he sniffed a lamppost.

'Do you know all the dogs in the area,
just based on their . . . leavings?' I asked.

'Most of them,' Lucky replied. 'There's
one particular dog I just can't identify, and
let's just say he's quite prolific . . .'

'How do you know it's a he?' I asked.

Lucky snorted. 'Female dogs don't tend
to aim so high. This fella can reach the
letter slot on a postbox.'

'I wish I hadn't asked,' I said.

I went back to thinking about what
Gran had said. About the true magic being
inside me. I didn't think she was just
talking about the crackling, fizzing tingle.

195

She was being more . . . mysterious than that.

Was she saying I needed to stop using my new powers? But she had said herself that I had a gift. Of course I had to use it.

I was Max the Magnificent, after all!

'I have to seize the day,' I said out loud. I had control of my powers now. I knew what I was doing. And there were only two days before Dad could lose his stall. There had to be a way to fix everything. That was why I'd been given these powers. I was sure of it!

'Did you just say you had to feed the dog?' Lucky said.

'No, I did not,' I said. 'Anyway, you've just had a muffin!'

'You don't know what it's like being a dog,' Lucky said. 'I'm always hungry!'

'I don't believe you,' I replied. 'You're just greedy.'

Still bickering, we turned down the little alley that's a shortcut between Cutler Street and Houndsditch, but I was so distracted I didn't notice that there was someone in there waiting for me.

'Max,' Lucky hissed. 'I think we should go another way.'

There was something in his voice that woke me from my thoughts.

I stopped and looked up, seeing the

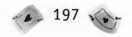

yellow coat instantly. I glanced down at Lucky to see his tail had curled downward.

'Max,' Lucky whispered as Bottley came stalking towards us, grinning in his mean way, 'let's go.'

But I didn't go. Not this time.

This time I'm not going to let him corner me, I thought. It was time to stand and face him.

'I've been watching you, Mullers,' he said menacingly. 'I don't know what's going on with you, but whatever it is, I want to get myself a piece of it.'

'I don't know what you're talking about,' I said sullenly.

'You've got some new magic tricks,'
he said. 'I saw you making illusions. I
saw you reading minds. I even saw you
take some bloke's wallet.'

I gasped. I hadn't realised Bottley
had been there when that had happened.
He must have followed me and Stretch
from the churchyard.

'I don't know how you're doing it
and I don't really care,' he said. 'And
I'm not going to say anything to anyone,
as long as you get me a wallet or two,
stuffed with cash.'

So that's what he wanted. Money.
Just like with the pound coins behind
the ear.

 199

No curiosity. No wonder. No interest in the magic. Just money.

Well, not this time, I thought. Today the worm turns.

I took a deep breath and concentrated hard as the tingling feeling built in my chest. I could do this. I had the power. I had the control, since Sophie had helped me to learn.

As Bottley stood watching me, I saw him flinch. He looked down at his trouser pocket, which had suddenly swelled up. He made as if to put his hand in there, but before he could do so, something popped out. Something pink and slimy and wriggly.

It was a worm.

But not an ordinary worm. It was a massive, huge, GIGANTIC worm. And it was getting bigger. It came coiling out, tearing Bottley's trouser pocket as it stretched up and wrapped itself around his body. His eyes bulged out like they were on stalks, and his face became a mask of terror. I grinned as Bottley's mouth opened in a silent scream. And then I saw my opportunity. I twitched my fingers and the worm's head shot forward.

Doosh!

Right inside Bottley's mouth.

Bottley fell to the ground, fighting against the disgusting creature as it squirmed.

 201

'What's the matter, Bottley?' I said. 'I thought you liked worms!'

'Max,' Lucky barked. 'Stop it! You're hurting him.' He ran up and seized my trouser leg in his teeth, pulling me away.

'Good,' I said fiercely. 'He thinks he can go around hurting other people. Well, now he's seeing what it feels like. Get off, Lucky!' I turned and pushed him away.

'You've made your point,' Lucky said, backing off. 'You're better than him. Now stop this!'

'You don't know anything, Lucky,' I snapped. 'Bottley deserves everything he gets.'

I looked back to Bottley, but the illusion had broken. He scrambled to his feet and legged it down the alley.

'You're a freak, Mullers,' he shouted as he ran. 'I'm going to tell.'

I grinned. 'Keep running, Worm Boy!' I yelled. 'No one will believe you!'

'Max . . .' Lucky was saying.

I turned to him, the crackling energy still coursing through me, filling me with giddy excitement.

'This isn't you,' Lucky said, shaking his head.

 203

At first I didn't know what he was on about. But as the power of the magic drained away again, I saw everything my friends had been seeing.

What Stretch had seen when I pinched the wallet.

What Sophie had seen when I cheated at the history quiz.

And what Lucky had just seen when I was bullying Bottley.

Because that's exactly what I had been doing.

Bullying.

'This is what Gran was trying to tell me, wasn't it?' I said, suddenly understanding. My legs felt weak. 'That I have to know when not to use my power.'

'She wasn't saying you shouldn't use your gifts,' Lucky explained. 'She was saying you have to be careful how and when you use them. And why.'

I squatted down and clutched my head in my hands, groaning.

'I'm an idiot!' I said. 'I thought I had all the answers, but I've learned nothing.'

'Don't be too hard on yourself, Max,' Lucky said, stepping forward and nuzzling me.

I hugged him tightly. 'I should use my gifts to help people,' I said, suddenly feeling like I was the worst person in the world. 'To make things better. To fix

things. Not to steal, or cheat, or bully. I'm a terrible person. What have I done?'

But Lucky was shaking his head. 'You're not a terrible person, Max. You're just learning lessons, like everyone else.' He licked my hand gently.

I thought back to what Mum had read in my horoscope. Seize the day.

But what did that mean?

It certainly didn't mean I should go round causing chaos and hurting people. It meant I had to take control. Control of my powers, control of myself. I was in charge and I needed to make the decisions. The right decisions.

'From now on,' I said solemnly, 'I will

only use my powers for good.'

'I'm pleased to hear it,' said Lucky.

'No stealing, only giving,' I went on. 'And no hurting, only helping. That's my code.'

'A boy needs a code,' Lucky agreed.

'Thanks for helping me to see what an idiot I was being,' I said, stroking his head.

'No problem,' Lucky replied. 'And speaking of giving and helping, I'm very, very hungry right now.'

'Then let's go home,' I said. 'Waggy Boy tonight. And it's beef.'

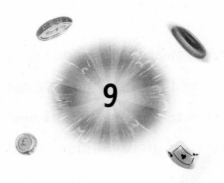

9

Grief Encounter

So basically I'd had a wake-up call.

I was determined that from now on I would be more responsible with my magic powers. And the next day I managed to do just that. I didn't read any teachers' minds, I resisted the temptation to make an illusion of a five-pound note at the cafeteria to buy doughnuts for me and my friends, and in PE I decided against using my telekinesis to blast a thundercrack wonder goal from the halfway line. Bottley kept his distance from me all day. I sort of felt bad about the worm thing. But I have to be honest, I didn't feel bad that he was avoiding me.

Yet as usual it seemed that Max Magic wasn't allowed to have a good day. There always had to be something that went wrong.

It was after school and I was on the stall. Dad had gone off for his tea. Things had been going well. We were selling teddy bears, which had been doing surprisingly

good numbers lately, and Dad had been talking about buying another batch from the wholesaler in Shoreditch. That was only going to happen if we could find some way to pay off the Crayfish Twins though. If we couldn't do that, then it was goodbye teddy bears and goodbye stall.

The thing about the teddy bears was that they came without stuffing, to save money on shipping. So Dad, Susie, Chris, Vinny and I would have to sit in front of the telly and stuff them for hours so Dad and I could sell them the next day. It was kind of fun for a while, but as time went on you got stuffing up your nose, in your ears, down the back of your neck and in your belly button. Until it seemed like it was the bears stuffing you rather than the other way around.

Anyway, they were selling OK and I spent the whole time keeping up the patter. I had a big supply of teddy-bear jokes.

'Why did Tigger stick his head down the toilet? He was looking for Pooh,' I called to a passing man, who laughed, but didn't buy a bear.

An old lady came up to inspect the teddies.

'Why do pandas like old movies?' I asked her. She shrugged. 'Cos they're black and white.' She laughed and bought one.

'Why did the bear cross the road?' I

called out with a grin. 'Chicken's day off.'

Things were going great. I had a roll of five-pound and ten-pound notes from the sales. Dad would be delighted. I didn't need to use my powers to sell teddy bears. All I needed was my natural charm and an endless supply of terrible jokes.

Then suddenly there they were.

The Crayfish Twins.

Right in front of me.

My heart sank. Gary held a big bag and seemed to be wearing a new suit. Barry stared at me with narrow eyes. In a flash, the crowds had melted away. No one wanted to be around when the Crayfish

Twins were in the area. I quickly slipped the roll of notes into my back pocket.

Barry opened his mouth to speak, but his brother got there first.

'Nice stall you've got here,' Gary said. 'It would be a shame if nothing happened to it.'

'Something!' Barry hissed.

'What?'

'It would be a shame if **something** happened to it,' Barry said impatiently. 'Not nothing. How many times have we been over this?'

'Oh yeah, sorry,' Gary said.

'Where's your old man then?' Barry growled at me.

 213

'He's having his dinner,' I explained.

'What's he having?' Gary asked.

'Um, chops, I think,' I said.

'Nice dinner, chops,' Gary said. 'Be a shame if something happened to them.'

'Like what?' I asked.

'Like . . .' Gary stopped to think. 'Like if someone overcooked them or something.'

Barry shot him a look. 'Let me do the talking,' he hissed, then turned back to me. 'Have you got my money, Master Mullers?'

I shook my head nervously.

'I'm curious,' Barry said. 'What exactly was it that you slipped into your back pocket as we approached?'

'It . . . it was my handkerchief,' I said.

I reached behind me and, from my sleeve, hidden from view, I pulled a brightly coloured string of  handkerchiefs, which I displayed with a nervous grin.

'How did you do that?!' Gary exclaimed, with a look of delight.

Barry gave him a dirty glance, then turned back to me. 'I think I'll take the roll of notes you've got back there.'

Sighing, I took out the money and looked at it. That was all the money I'd

just made, plus the float that Dad had left with me. Fifty pounds!

But what else could I do? I handed it over. Gary unsnapped the big catches at the top of his leather bag and opened it. I saw that it was full of cash. There must have been thousands and thousands in there. Barry counted the money I'd given him carefully and then added it to the bag.

'Shut it then, shut it!' he snapped at Gary, who was taking his time.

Barry looked around nervously until the bag was safely closed. Then he took out a small notebook and scribbled in it.

'Very nice,' he said. 'Now you only owe us £250.'

'What?!' I cried. 'I just gave you fifty quid. We owed £250 two days ago, so how can we still owe £250?'

'Interest,' Barry said with a wink. 'Twenty-five pounds a day until we get everything that's owed to us.'

I fumed. But I was helpless. This was just like Dad was saying. They would keep coming back for more and more. That's the problem with bullies. They don't stop until you stand up to them.

But what could I do? I couldn't use my magic powers to hurt people – I was absolutely sure about that. I couldn't cheat or steal either. So what was the answer?

'And remember,' Barry said with a mean

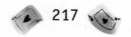

217

look in his eye, 'you've only got one more day. This time tomorrow it's payday.'

After they'd gone I tried to drum up some more interest in the teddy bears, but my heart wasn't in it. The encounter with the twins had really knocked me for six.

When Dad came back, I explained what had happened.

'I'm sorry,' I sniffed, nearly in tears. 'I didn't know what to do.'

He knelt and gave me a hug. 'It's not your fault,' he whispered. 'They're wrong'uns, the pair of them. And you did the right thing.'

'Gary had a big bag full of money,' I said. 'They have so much, and we have nothing. It's not fair, Dad!'

He knelt down and gave me a big bear hug. I could smell his aftershave. 'It's going to be all right, Max,' he said, and patted me gently on the back.

But as he pulled away I glimpsed a look on his face that told me he didn't really believe that.

He didn't believe it at all.

I felt a bit better when I got to Gran's shop. That place always makes me feel happy. And today she'd been baking shortbread, my favourite. Lucky greeted me enthusiastically.

'You seem very pleased to see me,' I said, giving him a hug.

'Gran said I wasn't allowed any shortbread until you arrived,' he explained.

'You don't . . . you don't talk to Gran when I'm not around, do you?' I asked.

'No,' he replied. 'Can't get a word in edgewise.'

As we munched on shortbread and sipped milk, I told Gran about my problems.

'The Crayfish family have been terrorising people in the market for decades,' Gran said, frowning. 'Back in the sixties my old man had a run-in with them. Some things just don't change. Those twins, they were always wrong'uns,

even when they were kids. The first time
the two of 'em was arrested it was for
stealing a calendar.'

'What happened?'

'They got six months each,' Gran
finished, cackling at her own joke.

'Gran, this is serious.'

'Sorry,' she said. 'Couldn't resist.'

'Why can bullies push people around
like that?' I asked. 'The world is so
unfair.'

'It can be,' she agreed, looking sad.

'Aren't you supposed to stand up to
bullies though?' I asked. 'Maybe it's time
someone . . .' I stumbled to a halt, not
wanting to say what I'd been thinking.

'Time someone blasted the bullies with a fireball?' Gran asked with a raised eyebrow.

'No,' I said. 'I know that's not right.'

'That's right, you don't want a barney,' Gran said.

'Barney?'

'It means fighting,' Gran said. 'Barney Rubble: trouble.'

'Who's Barney Rubble?' I asked, still confused.

'Someone from a long time ago,' Gran said.

'So that's it?' I said, frustrated. 'We just give in and let them take what they want? Is there really nothing we can do?'

'There's always something you can do,'

Gran said. 'Remember what I told you yesterday. You have something very special inside you, Max. And you must choose carefully how you use it.'

I looked at her closely. Once again I found myself wondering. Did she know about Arthur Andrews's chest? About my powers?

'As long as you're helping people, and not hurting them, then you can't go far wrong,' Gran said. 'That's the key.'

Then the bell tinkled and she shuffled off to see to the customer. But she stopped in the doorway and turned back to me.

'Here's what I think,' she said. 'I think there's a wind of change coming. And it's

 223

the younger generation that are going to bring it about. It's you and your friends, the good ones, the ones with the kind hearts and the open minds and the generosity. You're going to make this a better world.' And she left.

Lucky and I sat there, thinking over what Gran had said. About the wind of change. About using my powers not to hurt people but to help them.

And then I had an idea. It was risky, but I thought it might just work. And if everything went right, no one would get hurt.

10

Plans Aplenty

As soon as we got home, I set up a group video call with the gang. We had things to discuss.

'First of all,' I began, 'we need to raise £250 by tomorrow. Otherwise my dad will have to sell our stall.'

Daisy frowned. 'There's no way we

 225

can do that,' she said.

Sophie shook her head. 'In this
economy?'

Stretch looked confused. 'Is there even
that much money in the world?'

Lucky jumped up on the bed at that
point and peered at the laptop screen,
getting in the way. I pushed him aside.

'I knew I could count on you guys.' I
sighed. 'Look, we all need to get into the
ideas kitchen.'

Daisy was puzzled. 'The ideas kitchen?'

'Yeah. We need to take the issue out
of the problem fridge and put it in the
solution oven,' I said. 'And whack that
baby up to 200 degrees fan. We need

money, is what I'm saying.'

'What are you on about?' Lucky said, shaking his head.

'None of us have any money,' Sophie was saying. 'If it was that easy to raise £250 in a day, then don't you think we would have done it before?'

'We didn't have my powers before,' I pointed out.

'Of course!' Daring Daisy said. 'We could use your telekinesis to smash our way into the Bank of England and steal a million pounds.'

'You could go to a casino and read the minds of the other players in a high-stakes poker game,' Sophie said, her eyes bright.

'You could just create an illusion of the £250,' Stretch suggested.

Everyone paused.

'Am I on mute?' he asked.

'No, we heard,' I said. 'That's actually a really good idea.'

'Much better than mine,' Daisy agreed. 'Less violent.'

'I told you you weren't a dummy,' Sophie added. 'I think the timer on the ideas oven has just gone **ping**.'

Stretch looked really pleased.

'But I'm afraid it's not going to work,' I said. 'I'm not going to use my powers to steal the money, or to cheat anyone out of their money, and I'm not going to give the

Crayfish Twins an illusion that'll disappear as soon as I look away.'

I went on. 'Now, I need each of you to put on your thinking cap and come up with some ways of making real money. And if you could do it really quickly, that would be great. We don't have a lot of time left.'

'Well, what's **your** plan?' Sophie asked.

'Still working on my bit,' I said. 'But the first part is that tomorrow we all have to bunk off school.'

'Great,' Daisy said.

'I'm loving this plan already,' Stretch agreed.

Sophie frowned. 'Is that necessary?'

she asked. She hated missing school. But when she saw my face she sighed and nodded.

'I'll meet you all down the market first thing tomorrow morning,' I said.

I came downstairs the next morning with a bright smile, flipping a deck of cards from one hand to the other. Susie was chatting on her phone and twirling her hair. Dad and Vinny were arguing about who was West Ham's best-ever right-back. Chris had pulled the toaster to pieces and was inspecting it.

'Is the toaster not working?' I asked.

'It was before he pulled it apart!' Mum said, exasperated.

'What does my horoscope say today?' I asked.

She smiled and peered at the paper in front of her, squinting. I concentrated hard, feeling the tingling in my chest. I saw the words on the page. I concentrated harder. The letters rearranged themselves into different patterns.

Mum frowned, read the horoscope again and then read it out loud. 'Aries should avoid school today. No good can come of it.' She looked up at me, her expression puzzled and more than a little alarmed.

'What?!' I said in a shocked voice.

 231

'But I absolutely **must** go to school today. I need to learn!'

Mum read the horoscope for a fourth time. 'Sorry, Max,' she said. 'The stars must not be trifled with. I don't think you should go to school.'

'Well . . . darn it,' I said, trying not to grin. I shook my head in feigned distress. 'What a terrible, terrible shame.'

'Don't overdo it,' Lucky growled.

An hour later I was down the market, wearing my hat, in front of Astral Alice's Tent of Telling. Daisy had texted us to tell us where to meet. She had had an idea.

In fact all three of them had had ideas.
Daisy's and Stretch's were really good.
Sophie wouldn't give me the details of hers
yet. I just hoped it was as clever as she
was.

'It's so early,' Stretch said. 'I haven't
even had my second pot of tea yet.'

'Alice never gets here before 10 a.m.,'
Daisy explained. 'That gives us an hour.'

 233

'An hour to do what?' Sophie asked.

'To read some minds,' Daisy said. 'And get our palms crossed with silver. We'll have to put on a good show though, just like Alice does. She has lights and smoke and ectoplasm for the atmosphere, and spooky music and sound effects. It's all part of the show.'

'OK. Who does what?' I asked.

'You read the minds,' Daisy said, 'Sophie can do the spooky noises and Stretch can do the lights.'

'And what about you?' I asked.

'Well, you don't really look like an Alice,' she said to me as she put on a colourful headscarf.

I grinned. 'Brilliant!'

Sophie groaned as we entered the tent. 'I'm missing double geography for this?'

But she soon got into it and gave me and Daisy a microphone each.

'Make sure you talk into this,' she'd said. 'I'll put some ghostly effects over your voice.'

Ten minutes later, we had our first customer.

It was a lady about Mum's age, with a red face and a strong jaw. She sat down and glared at Daisy.

From where I was hiding behind a screen I could see Daisy gulp. But we

 235

don't call her Daring Daisy for nothing!
She put on a spooky voice. Through the
microphone Sophie had rigged, it made
her voice sound deep and mysterious, with
growly background noises.

Stretch dimmed the lights and made
patterns swirl on the inside of the
backdrop. It was really effective. I'd
wondered about throwing in a few illusions,
but I didn't need to. Sophie and Stretch
had it covered!

'What do you look for?' Daisy intoned.
'What needs to be found? I will help you.
If you give us five pound.'

'I'm looking for my wedding ring,' the
lady said, sitting down. 'It disappeared

about a week ago. Can't think what I could
have done with it. I just want it back.'
Sophie nodded and cast a quick glance over
at me, half hidden behind the screen. The
customer couldn't see me, but Daisy could.

'I'll try to make contact with my spirit
walker,' she said, glancing at me. 'His
name is um . . . Guruluru . . . um . . .
guru.'

'Guruluru-Umguru?' the woman said,
frowning.

'Yes. It's a common name in . . . um,
the astral plane.'

The woman shrugged. 'OK.'

Daisy went on. 'I'm sure Guruluru-
Umguru will be able to look inside your

 237

mind and help you remember what you did with the ring.' She winked at me.

I started to concentrate, letting my mind expand, thinking about the ring. It came to me almost immediately.

'I have found it,' I whispered into the microphone. My voice came hissing through the hidden speakers in the room. The lady looked startled, as did Daisy for that matter. Stretch had put all sorts of special effects on the audio and I really did sound like a spirit walker called Guruluru-Umguru.

'Is it in my house?' the woman asked, breathlessly. 'The garden? At work?'

'No,' I said. 'It's down the pawnbroker's.'

'The pawnbroker's?' the woman asked, puzzled.

'Oh yes,' I whispered. 'Your husband sold it so he could put a bet on the greyhounds.'

'Gambling again!' the woman cried, her face even redder. 'He promised me he'd given up!'

'He hasn't,' I hissed breathily.

'I'll kill him!' the woman shrieked, and stood to go.

Daisy snapped back to life. 'Er, that will be five pounds, please.'

The woman threw a five-pound note on the table and rushed out, muttering.

'That was really stressful,' Sophie

 239

said, her face flushed. 'That poor woman.'

I shrugged. 'She wanted to find her ring and now she has.'

'But how did you know where the ring was from reading her mind?' Stretch asked. 'She didn't know her husband had stolen it.'

'I didn't read her mind,' I explained. 'I read her husband's mind.'

'Her husband?' Daisy was confused.

'Yeah, he's waiting for her outside the tent.' Just then there was a thump and a howl of pain from the street.

'How could you?!' the woman yelled.

Then the tent flap was flung open and

we turned in shock to see Astral Alice
staring at us.

'You're early!' I sputtered.

'I came straight away when I knew this
was going on,' she said. 'Saw it in my tea
leaves.'

'LEG IT!' Daisy yelled, and we did.
Out through the back of the tent and away
down through the market, pursued by a
furious Astral Alice.

'Right,' I said, once we'd reached a
safe distance. Alice couldn't run fast
in her swirly robes. 'How much have we
got?'

'Five pounds,' Sophie said. 'Only £245
to go.'

 241

'Holy moly,' Stretch said. 'Earning money is hard.'

'It's gonna get harder,' I said. 'You're up next.'

11

Teapot Trauma

We used the five pounds to buy a set of crockery. Saucers, cups, plates and a shiny teapot.

'This is madness,' Sophie said. 'You've just spent all our capital. We should have invested that money.'

'We are investing,' I said. 'We're

investing in Stretch. Have some faith.'

We chose a likely spot on a corner and
Stretch stood apart, stretching and flexing.
I'd seen him do this before; he knew
exactly what he had to do.

'Saucer first, please, Max,' he said. I
flipped a saucer up at him and he caught it
neatly on his forearm. This brought a bit of
attention and a couple of people stopped
to watch. I followed it up with a teacup.
Stretch shifted position a bit and the teacup
plopped onto the saucer and stuck there.
I quickly followed up with three more
saucers, which Stretch caught on his arms.
Then three more cups plopped onto the
saucers, 1-2-3.

A few people laughed and the crowd grew.

Finally I threw the teapot. But I got a bit overexcited and the 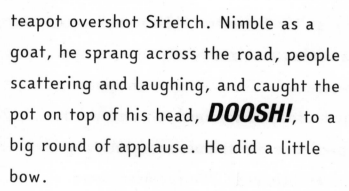 teapot overshot Stretch. Nimble as a goat, he sprang across the road, people scattering and laughing, and caught the pot on top of his head, **DOOSH!**, to a big round of applause. He did a little bow.

I grinned as I watched Stretch tilt his head forward. A stream of steaming tea poured out and splashed into one of

 245

the cups. Quickly and carefully he filled the other three cups, then offered them to some of the people in the crowd, who accepted happily. Who doesn't love a cup of tea in the East End of London?

I stepped forward. 'Ladies and gentlemen, please can we have a round of applause for Sebastian "Stretchy" Cross and his amazing magical tea set!'

There was a huge round of applause. Stretch stepped forward to acknowledge the applause but tripped and fell, a look of alarm on his face. The crowd gasped as the teapot went flying. But without missing a beat Stretch did a perfect forward roll and came back up onto his feet.

The teapot landed neatly on his head.

A beat passed, then the crowd erupted into cheers. I walked around with my hat out and pretty much everyone dropped a few coins in until it was heavy with the weight.

'Brilliant!' Daring Daisy said as we reassembled. 'You were amazing, Stretch.'

'How much help did you give him with your magic, Max?' Sophie asked.

'None at all,' I said. 'I was there ready to lend a hand if something went wrong, but Stretch did all that by himself.'

Everyone patted Stretch on the back and he grinned like a Cheshire cat.

'Right,' I said. 'Let's wait for the crowd

to clear and then we'll go again, yeah?'

'Go again where?' a new voice said from behind us. We spun to see the unwelcome face of . . .

'PC Peaceful!' I groaned.

PC Peaceful was our local police officer. He was well-named because all he was interested in was keeping things quiet. He liked to chat (quietly) but he didn't do an awful lot else.

'I heard news of a disturbance, Mr Mullers,' PC Peaceful said. 'Some unlicensed selling going on, distracting the punters from the stalls what pay their rates. You wouldn't happen to know anything about that, would you?'

I frowned at him. 'Why are you having a go at us?' I asked. 'We're just trying to make some honest money. Not like the Crayfish Twins. They're the real crooks. Why don't you go after them?'

PC Peaceful looked a bit taken aback at this. He looked around, as if expecting the Crayfish Twins to suddenly appear behind him.

'Look,' he said, 'it's my job to keep the peace, right. I like a nice, calm market with no trouble and no noise.'

'Or maybe you're just frightened of them,' Daisy suggested.

'I'm not frightened. I'm just waiting for them to slip up,' PC Peaceful said weakly.

 249

'Then I've got them, right?'

I sighed.

'Now sling your hook,' the policeman said, suddenly confident again. 'I don't want to see you round here for the rest of the day.'

'How much have we got?' Sophie asked as we wandered off.

'Forty-three pounds,' I said glumly. 'We're miles off.'

'Don't worry,' Sophie said, making a note in her Business Book. 'I've got this.'

'You?' Daisy asked. 'I thought you said this was all a waste of time.'

'You thought we should be at school,'
Stretch pointed out.

'Hey, we're a team, remember,' Sophie
replied, 'even if I think you lot don't always
make the best choices. We're all in this
together, and I'll support you all the way.'

'That's really kind,' I said. 'Thanks,
Sophie.'

'Right, so give me all the money,' she
said.

'What?'

'You have to spend money to make
money,' she said. She saw the look of
doubt on my face. 'Trust me, Max,' she
said, waving her notebook. 'I've done my
research and I know exactly how we can turn

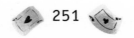

forty-three pounds into two hundred and fifty. First we've got to get down to the wholesaler.'

'Teddy bears?!' Daisy cried.

'Oh no,' I said.

'These aren't ordinary teddy bears,'

Sophie said. 'Apparently these are the latest thing off the telly.' Stretch gasped as he saw what Sophie was carrying. 'That's a MegaTed 9000!'

he cried. 'They're armour-plated and carry KillZap guns.'

'Why does a teddy bear need armour and a gun?' Daisy asked.

'To battle the evil Kthulge Empire,' Stretch explained. 'You must have heard the MegaTed 9000 theme song?' He sang:

'If you go down to the woods today,
      you're in for a big surprise.
If you go down to the woods today,
      you're sure to be vaporised.'

'Kids these days,' Daisy said, shaking her head.

'You still have to stuff them though,

253

don't you?' I said. 'The bears?'

I could feel my neck starting to itch already. But I knew Sophie was right. The teddy bears did make a big profit; Dad had told me that. And these MegaTed bears were pretty cool.

Sophie handed another two huge bags of stuffing to Stretch, who was already wobbling under the weight of four.

'Each empty MegaTed 9000 bear suit costs 40p,' Sophie said. 'The stuffing is only 10p per bear. And each bear sells for five pounds. That's a 900 per cent markup.'

'Is that right?' Daisy asked, looking at Stretch. 'Nine hundred per cent sounds like a lot.'

Stretch shrugged. 'I can't do sums without counting on my fingers,' he said, 'and I'm holding all these bags.' Then he looked thoughtful and added, 'Also, I don't think I've got enough fingers.'

'Don't look at me,' I said. 'I can't even do sums with my fingers.'

'All we have to do,' Sophie went on, 'is get the stuffing into the bears, then sell them on Max's stall while his dad is having his dinner.'

'You're a genius!' I said.

'I know,' Sophie replied, and dumped a big bag of empty teddy-bear suits into my arms. 'Now, who knows a quiet place where we can get to work?'

'My house is empty at this time of day,' I said.

Half an hour later we were sitting in my living room. Only now I wasn't quite so sure about Sophie being a genius.

There was stuffing everywhere. All four of us were coughing and spluttering, and it didn't matter how many cups of tea Stretch made us. Lucky, unable to stop sneezing, had left us to it and was hiding under my bed. We'd only managed to do one teddy bear so far and his armour was a bit lumpy and his KillZap gun hung limp.

'It's not as easy as I thought,' Sophie admitted. 'I'm starting to understand why the markup on teddy bears is so high. It's all the labour that goes into stuffing them.' She made a note in her little Business Book.

I looked at the clock. It was 3 p.m.

'We're never going to finish these in time,' Daisy said. 'You have to be on the stall in two hours – it'll take us that long just to clear up the mess.'

Stretch sneezed. 'And we've spent all the money now.'

'We tried our best,' Daisy said, coughing up a bit of stuffing. 'But . . .'– cough – 'it's just not possible.'

'Anything is possible!' I insisted. 'We can't give up now. If we don't get that

 257

money to the Crayfish Twins before 6 p.m., then my dad will have to sell his stall!'

'We want to help, Max,' Sophie said. 'But there just isn't enough time. We can't make the bears fast enough. We'd need a whole production line.'

I looked up at her. 'What did you just say?'

'I said we'd need a production line. You know, like in a factory.'

I looked down at the lumpy MegaTed on my lap, and suddenly I knew what I needed to do. We'd got this far just on brains and hard work, but now something else was called for.

A little bit of Max Magic!

My fingers tingled. My chest tingled. I put the bear down on the floor and concentrated.

A few seconds later, the bear twitched. Then it sat up and looked around. Stretch gasped as it got to its feet, slung its KillZap gun over its shoulder and marched over to the pile of empty bear suits. It took one off the top, turned and walked unsteadily over to the open bag of stuffing.

Then the first bear began to stuff the second.

'Oh wow!' Daisy said.

We all watched in silence as the bear completed the job. It took about ten minutes, and the bear did it all perfectly.

 259

The new bear was stuffed as well as if it had been done by a machine.

'Unbelievable,' I breathed.

Then both bears marched back to the pile of bear suits and each grabbed one more, taking it to the bag of stuffing and starting the process all over again.

'A bear production line,' Daisy said.

'Max, you're the Henry Ford of stuffed toys,' Sophie said.

'Henry who?' Daisy asked.

'Henry Ford – he made cars,' Sophie said. 'Lots of them. He invented the idea of the production line.'

'And he used bears?' Stretch asked, confused.

Just then Lucky came back in to see what was going on. He took one look at the bears wandering about the place and leaped at one, barking and growling, his hackles raised.

'No, Lucky,' I cried, dragging him away.

'They're bears,' he said as I shut him in the kitchen. 'I have to protect you.'

'They're just toys,' I sighed.

'They have **guns**, Max,' he whined.

Within an hour, we had fifty stuffed toys. Actually fifty-one. There must have been an extra in the bag. I decided the original bear, the lumpy one, probably

 261

wasn't fit for sale so I gave it to Stretch.

'Great!' he said. 'I can order it to make me cups of tea.'

'Will the bears keep their magic forever?' Sophie asked me in a whisper.

'I don't know,' I said. 'I started them off using telekinesis, but they seem to be doing their own thing now. Maybe they only move when I'm nearby. I guess we'll find out!'

We let Lucky out, but first I made him promise not to attack the bears. He agreed reluctantly and eyed them suspiciously as they marched about, doing drills and weapons practice.

'Right,' I said, coughing up a bit of foam, 'now for the next part of the plan. This is going to be the tricky bit.'

12

Bear Battalion

Dad gave me a funny look as I arrived at the stall.

'You up to something?' he asked as the Bow Bells started to chime.

I shook my head. 'Me? Why would you say that?'

'It's just that you're on time,' he said.

'And you have yellow fluff all over your clothes.' He took my top hat off. 'And in your hair! Is that stuffing?'

'Dunno what you're talking about,' I said. I sneezed.

He sighed. 'Look, just keep out of trouble, will you? And if those Crayfish Twins come sniffing about, tell them I'll see them after I've had my tea.'

'Do you have the money?' I asked.

He shook his head. 'I'm going to talk to them,' he said. 'Try and make them see reason. I'm going to ask for more time to pay. It's no good for anyone if I'm forced to sell up.'

'But, Dad,' I said, 'they might hurt you.'

 265

'Don't worry about me, Max,' he said with what I think was supposed to be a reassuring smile. But I could see through him. I knew he was worried. But if my plan went well, then he'd never have to worry about the Crayfish Twins ever again.

'Anyway,' he said, 'just keep out of trouble, OK?'

I nodded. 'Just a nice quiet shift in the market,' I said.

'No knocking over stalls, no cumin clouds, no acrobatics, none of your magic tricks, OK?'

'Definitely no magic **tricks**,' I said.

He eyed me suspiciously for a moment longer, but then I heard his tummy rumble, and he ruffled my hair, plopped my hat back on my head and went off in the direction of home.

I waited for a few minutes until I was sure the coast was clear. Then I took a deep breath, felt for the chest tingle, stuck my fingers in my mouth and gave the loudest, clearest whistle you ever heard.

A few people looked over at me, but for a while nothing happened. I frowned. Had something gone wrong? Had I suddenly lost my powers? Were the bears too far away for my telekinesis to work?

But then I heard it. The sound of a drum and a penny whistle. And under it, the faint padding of one hundred little feet.

 267

The crowds parted, and right down the middle of Petticoat Lane came an army of fifty MegaTed 9000 bears. Two abreast, chests puffed out, stuffed full to bursting, with armoured vests and helmets on, marching proud and tall . . . well, proud and short. I was relieved to see they'd left their guns at home.

Daisy was on the right of the column with a whistle. Stretch was on the left with a little drum. Sophie brought up the rear. And leading the column, walking stiffly with head held high, was none other than Lucky.

The crowd loved it.

Lucky barked and the teddy bears came to a stop, right in front of the stall. He looked up at me and whispered, 'All present and correct, sir. These bears certainly are disciplined, I'll give them that.'

I took a deep breath, adjusted my top hat and jumped up onto the trestle table.

'Ladies and gentlemen,' I cried out, 'my dog Lucky there – a very clever dog indeed. I bought him off a blacksmith, don't you know? As soon as I got him home, he made a bolt for the door.'

The crowd laughed and came closer. They weren't sure what was going on here, but they could tell there was a bit of fun coming their way. I saw Mr Ponsonby, the local vicar, at the front, grinning at me.

'Only joking,' I went on. 'I actually got Lucky from the market. The flea market.'

 269

Lucky gave me a hard stare.

'Now, ladies and gentlemen,' I cried, 'you've heard of a bare cheek. You've heard of a bare bum. I bet you ain't never heard of a bear army. But that's what we've got for you today!'

I waved a hand and the bears turned as one towards me and saluted.

'This is the very latest techno-mological development from Mullers Industries,' I went on. 'Genuine walking, talking MegaTed 9000 armour-plated bears who will follow your orders.'

I pointed at one of the bears, then to a man in the audience. 'You, bring me that bloke's hat.'

The teddy bear shot off and jumped up
onto the man's shoulders, snatching his
hat, to the delight of the crowd. The man
looked alarmed, but then he broke into a
grin and joined the applause as the bear
brought the hat to me.

I bowed, winked and frisbeed it back to its owner.

'You can even get them to help out around the house, give you a day off.'

I waved my hands and the bears sprang into action, with some grabbing a dustpan and brush, others picking up litter and one enterprising bear polishing the brasswork on Mr Cullins's bric-a-brac stall.

'They'll defend you from enemies,' I growled, and a squad of bears leaped into formation, surrounding the vicar, who looked alarmed and held up his hands in surrender. The crowd loved it.

'These little fellows can even dance a jig,' I cried.

Daisy and Stretch played a merry tune and the little bears started to dance around.

The crowd absolutely lost it at that point. There were cheers and roars of delight; people were literally rolling on the ground laughing.

'Now,' I said when the music had stopped and the crowd had settled slightly, 'as a special introductory offer, these bears, which would normally retail for £69.99, are available to the good people of Petticoat Lane for just five pounds each.'

They swamped me. It was chaos, a stampede! The stall collapsed under the weight as everyone leaned over, reached

across or climbed up, trying to get their hands on one of the magic bears. Every last MegaTed bear was sold within five minutes.

'Should have asked for more,' I groaned as Daisy, Sophie and Stretch helped me to my feet and dusted me off.

Then, 'Oh no!' I said, looking at the shattered stall and the scattered toys. 'Dad told me to keep out of trouble.'

'Did you sell them all?' Stretch asked.

'Oh. Yeah,' I said, counting the crumpled notes in my hand. 'Fifty bears, five pounds each, £250 in total.' Suddenly I didn't feel so bad about the stall. We could always mend it again – the money to pay off the Crayfish Twins was more important right now.

I waved the money in Stretch's face, grinning happily. '£250, Stretch – we did it!'

'Well, thank you very much,' a voice said behind me.

I turned, knowing exactly who it was. Barry Crayfish.

'I heard the disturbance and figured you'd be at the centre of it, Master Mullers. I was going to wait to speak to your father. But I see you have my money.'

'I have your money, Barry Crayfish,' I said coolly.

'Nice stall,' Gary said, pointing to our

stall, which was anything but nice at that moment, lying flat in the road with toys scattered everywhere. 'Shame if something, er, happened . . . Um, Barry, I think something **has** happened to their stall.'

'Never mind that!' Barry snapped. 'We're talking about the money Mr Mullers here owes us.'

'And I'll give it to you,' I said. 'I do owe it, because of Gary's suit. And that's fair. The Mullers always pay their debts.'

'I'm pleased to hear it,' Barry said. 'Now hand it over.'

'I will,' I said. 'But it's the last time anyone from my family gives money to you or your brother. Paying off a debt is one thing. Paying someone not to hurt you is something else altogether. And we're not doing it any more.'

Barry stiffened and his eyes narrowed. For a moment it looked like he might get really angry. I felt a faint tingle in my chest, and a breeze sprang up around us. But then he smiled, a nasty, slimy smile. 'Usually I'd break a man's arm if he spoke to me like that,' he said. He paused, staring at me with a look of venom.

I swallowed. Lucky growled.

'But you're young, Max Mullers,' he went on, 'and you clearly don't understand how the world works. Not yet, anyway. So I'll help you out with some free advice.'

 277

He took another step closer.

Lucky growled again.

I swallowed, but stood my ground.

'What you don't seem to understand,' he went on, 'is that you're not paying for nothing. You're paying for a service.'

'And what service is that exactly?' Sophie asked.

'Yes,' Gary said, frowning. 'To be honest, I've never been quite sure about that.'

'Why, keeping the peace, of course,' Barry said with an innocent smile.

The breeze strengthened, and a crisp packet spun along the Lane.

'No one likes noise and disorder and chaos, do they? We don't like it, you

don't like it, the punters don't like it.
PC Peaceful, he certainly doesn't like it.
So that's our role here, Mr Mullers. That's
what we bring to this marketplace. That's
what we sell. Peace!'

'And what if you don't bring peace?' I
said as I handed the £250 over.

Barry took the money and counted it.
Gary unclipped the big catches on the
brown bag. His new suit ruffled in the
stiffening breeze.

A wind of change is coming, Gran's
voice whispered to me.

'What if, instead of peace, you caused a
disturbance?' I asked. 'What would happen
then?'

'If that ever happens . . .' Barry said as he scribbled his note in his little black book:

£250 *from* M. *Mullers*.

The wind picked up more, and the canopies on the market stalls flapped, tugging at their restraints.

'. . . then it would be only right for PC Peaceful to handcuff us and take us off to the clink.'

'Yes. I thought that might be the case,' I said.

Then I took a deep breath, concentrated and . . .

LET. IT. RIP.

A mighty wind came howling through the narrow streets and lanes of old London. It whipped through the marketplace, sending people shouting and running for cover. It caught hats and dresses and coats. Piles of litter went swirling around, caught in eddies, spinning like a tornado of rubbish. People shouted and cried in alarm.

Barry looked around uncertainly. Lucky whined.

I breathed in deeper and the wind increased in strength. I watched a number of canopies tear free with a ripping sound and soar high in the air like colourful kites dancing in the sky.

'Holy roly-poly moly!' Stretch cried.

The Kumars' curry stall was dragged ten feet down the lane, hit a kerb and fell over on its side, sending spice powders flying into the air in great, colourful, sweet-smelling clouds that enveloped us like a sandstorm in the Sahara.

'CUMIN!' Gary howled, and he fell over backwards and dropped his brown leather bag, still wide open.

Instantly, hundreds and hundreds of banknotes came streaming out of the bag and went flying up into the sky.

'No, no!' Barry shouted, lurching around trying to snatch the money out of the air. He tripped over his sprawled brother and went down onto the cobbles.

'That's money!' someone yelled and, not needing any further invitation, the good people of Petticoat Lane Market swamped the scene, shrieking in excitement, reaching up, jumping, stretching to grab as many of the flying banknotes as they could.

'That's **my** money!' Barry screamed from where he lay in the road. 'I stole it fair and square!'

He scrambled to his feet, slipping on the cobbles in his desperation to save his precious money. He leaped and twirled like a ballet dancer, thrashing his arms about as he tried to snatch the fluttering notes out of the air.

As I breathed out the wind died and the notes came floating down, which only added to the excitement of the crowd, who milled around, stuffing their pockets with captured fivers, tens, twenties and fifties.

Then I saw Barry Crayfish striding towards me through the mob, a look of absolute fury on his face. He dragged his coughing brother along beside him, and from his back pocket, with his other hand, I saw him pull something out.

'He's got a knife!' Sophie shouted.

The crowd turned as one, someone screamed and then there was pandemonium.

Everyone scattered, leaving us alone with the Crayfish Twins.

Lucky barked angrily and moved in front of me.

'You are going to pay for that, Mullers!' Barry Crayfish snarled.

He held the knife out in front of him and took a step towards me.

Snick, went the sound of handcuffs snapping shut around Barry's wrist.

'Gotcha,' said PC Peaceful.

Gary sneezed, held up his hands to his face, and a second snick followed the first.

'You too,' PC Peaceful added.

'About time,' Daisy said.

'I told you,' PC Peaceful said, to us. 'I couldn't do anything until they crossed the line. Well, they've crossed it now.

And I think they'll be behind bars for a long time to come. That's the last time these two will disturb the peace around here.'

'It wasn't us,' Barry fumed. 'It was him. He was the one what disturbed the peace. With his magic wind.'

'Magic wind, eh?' PC Peaceful laughed, leading the twins away. 'That's a new one.

You should try that on the judge.'

I dropped to my knees and gave Lucky a hug. 'Thanks for defending me there, old chum,' I whispered.

'No problem, little buddy,' he replied.

I stood up. The crowd were still scrabbling around for money, and while their attention was elsewhere, I pointed a magic finger towards our stall. Sophie gasped as it quickly rebuilt itself. The scattered toys jumped up off the cobbles and came to rest back on the trestle table. The canopy snapped back into place.

'You're really getting the hang of that now,' she said with a grin.

'All thanks to you, and your lesson

plans,' I said. 'Maybe learning isn't such a waste of time after all.'

'You know we've got some more learning to do, don't you?' she asked.

I nodded. 'I know. We need to figure out what this is, this . . . magic,' I said. 'Where it comes from, what it means, and why me?'

'Yeah,' she said. 'And the first place to look is that old chest. Who was Arthur Andrews? Where did he travel? And what did he find there?'

'Well, that's a job for another day,' I said, looking around at the chaos in the Lane. 'Right now, I've got a bit of tidying up to do.'

'Shame we didn't get to grab any of that

money,' Daisy said ruefully as she wandered over.

'It'll all get spent again soon enough,' Sophie said. 'Basic monetary theory. Would you like me to explain about cash circulating through the local economy?'

'Maybe another time,' Stretch said.

'Actually,' I said, 'we do still have the £250. That's our money. We earned it, together.'

'No, you handed that over to the twins,' Stretch said. 'I saw you.'

I reached behind Stretch's ear and pulled out a tight roll of notes. 'I told you,' I said, grinning, 'Anything Is Possible.'

Learn How to Do Magic with Stephen Mulhern

Scan this QR code for
a step-by-step guide to the tricks
you are about to read – and
more UNBELIEVABLE magic . . .

Find out the all-important secrets
behind mastering these tricks so you
can entertain your friends and family!

Magical Mind-Reading

Stun your friends with your unbelievable mind-reading power – just tell them to follow these simple steps!

- Think of a number between 1 and 10.

- Double that number.

- Add 8.

- Halve the number.

- Subtract the first number you thought of.

- Find the letter for the number you're thinking of:

  A = 1 B = 2 C = 3 D = 4 E = 5 F = 6
  G = 7 H = 8 I = 9 J = 10

- Now think of a country beginning with that letter.

- Take the second letter of the country and think of an animal beginning with that letter.

- Now think of that animal's colour.

- *You don't get many grey elephants in Denmark, do you?*

How to Palm a Coin

1. Take a £2 coin in one hand.

2. Squeeze your thumb in so that you're gripping the coin.

3. Turn your hands over, palm down, without the coin dropping out.

4 Turn your hands so your palms face each other and pretend to throw the coin from one hand to the other, making a fist as if you have caught it.

> *Practise in front of a mirror.*

5 Open your empty fist to reveal . . . no coin! It seems as though the coin has vanished, but it never left the first hand.

6 Wave the hand holding the coin over the other hand, sneakily dropping the coin from one to the other, and then quickly close the hand now holding the coin into a fist. . .

7 Finally open your fist – the coin has reappeared!

> *Video yourself doing the trick and watch it back.*

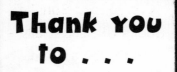

Thank you to . . .

My mum and dad, for all your support and for helping me believe in myself. Love you so so much.

Jamie, Susie, Chris and Vince, for everything that we have all achieved so far.

Amanda, Millie, Claire and Nads for all your commitment and hard work. 'You are the best, you are the management!!!'

Tom, what a journey this has been, and here is to a great future ahead.

Everyone at Bonnier Books UK, especially – Ruth, Talya, Dom, Marina, Rob, Eleanor, Jess, Kate and Steph. It's been a truly magical journey and Ruth, you have been incredible and your team have done us all proud!

Begoña, your art brings this book to life in the best possible way!

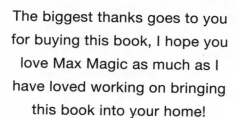

The biggest thanks goes to you for buying this book, I hope you love Max Magic as much as I have loved working on bringing this book into your home!

Tom Easton has published more than forty books for readers of all ages. He has written books about vampires, pirates, teenage girl boxers and teenage boy knitters (not all in the same book). He lives in Surrey with his wife and three children. You can find out more about him at **www.tomeaston.co.uk** or on Twitter @TomEaston

Begoña Fernández Corbalán was born and raised in a small town in Spain. As a child she loved to draw, and after finishing a degree in Fine Arts, she specialised in illustration. She works with watercolor, gouache and pencil as well as illustrating digitally.